QUARRY

for John Coates

Dive in. Turn to water before it freezes.

Nobody

I DIDN'T KNOW what a quarry was until I saw the one that would belong to us. A pit carved for mining. Dig what you need – the dynamite gap – leave a hole for evidence. Don't think about air filling it up. Air fills up everything. Water makes the quarry more than it is; the blue we were drawn to. On the dock, looking out. My mother on one side. My father, the other. Their big shoulders pressing me in.

It was our first summer living beside a lake that wasn't a lake, with wind tents of blue moving in the jewelled sunlight, up and gone and up again. The limestone, cut into jagged rock, layered with the weight of dead animals, ancient sea animals, imprints. Lush green trees, they surrounded as a forest. Dad had found the place by chance after spotting the For Sale sign outside a white gate that led to a long gravel driveway, a bend that led to a mini-lake, the house of Mom's dreams.

We made up dives that summer, me and Cindy. The Watermelon Dive—legs in a V. The About-to-Die Dive—a rambling, dramatic shotgun death off the dock. The Scissor Kick Dive—a flutter of pointed legs in the air. And the Drowning Dive—rise to the surface and float like the dead fish that smacked against the limestone rock, oozing decay's stink. With a two-year advantage, I gave my nine-year-old cousin a three-second head start whenever we raced off the dock to reach the floating raft. Sometimes a hit of the giggles cut through my determination—a memory of something we'd laughed about while lying in the dark, tucked in single beds, or while eating Rice Krispies, opening up our food-filled mouths to shout: *see-food diet!*

Mom served as judge as she sat on the dock smoking her brand, Benson & Hedges. She was there to rescue us if we were to drown. I knew this was an illusion. Though an athlete, Mom could barely swim and deep water scared her. She excelled at land games, sports with racquets like badminton and tennis, especially tennis. Our shelves of knick-knacks were stacked with gold trophies, tiny females frozen in mid-serve.

"Watch, Mom. Watch!"

"Caitlin Maharg, I'm always watching."

I dove and then Cindy dove and we made her grade us.

"Ten out of ten," said Mom.

"Me or Cindy?"

"Both." She lit another cigarette and exhaled the burst of smoke.

"Aw, Mom! Someone has to win."

Despite her fierce competitiveness on the tennis court and my constant pleading, she refused to budge. We always came out even.

When we got tired of diving, we swam like the darting sunfish, the smallest fish in the quarry.

Standing on tubes was something Cindy could do better than me. Her smaller build gave her an advantage. I could stand on an inner tube, no problem, but my balance wouldn't last like hers. My long legs wobbled like the egg-shaped Weebles we played with on the floor of Cindy's Burlington bedroom when we weren't spying on her two older brothers. My Uncle Jim's new job had brought the Brant family back to Ontario, all the way from Calgary. Because they'd been so far away, I'd never thought of them as family until now.

Dad didn't like to swim. When he did go in the water, to work the stress off himself or shampoo his grey-peppered hair, he stayed within arm's reach of the dock ladder. Because his arm was so long, like all of his limbs, he looked farther away than he really was.

When the water was still, you could see rock bottom. But you couldn't touch it, not off the dock – feet had no resting place. On clear, windless days we watched the carp suspended below, like sunken logs or torpedoes. They never did anything. In fact it was us that scared them, our manic splashes getting in and out of the water, our specialized dives. After the water settled again, Cindy and I would try to find them, but they'd long disappeared.

Sunfish never scared. Surface swimmers, they hovered by the dock with the constant hope of being fed. Desperate nibblers, they mouthed anything, including Mom's cigarette butts, though they always spat them out. Sometimes we felt them nibbling our toes – a safe sensation when we sat on the dock and could see the source of the gummy tickle, but when it happened inside the quarry, as we treaded water or floated on our backs, the *Jaws* theme song ran through my head, and I imagined the deadly ones – catfish with snake-like whiskers, serpent-shaped muskie with sharp teeth or the turtle with the jaw that could snap your big toe off.

The quarry wasn't always stocked with fish. There were no nearby rivers or tributaries to lead bass, sunfish, perch and more to the lake-sized pit. Dad said previous owners had put them there. And because there were few predators, each species grew in number, including the deadly ones. But Cindy and I were pretty good at waving away the darker things. We had each other and a mother able to watch us.

When Dad came home from work those summer evenings, he watched us too. Barefooted and bare-chested in his blue swimming trunks, he was eager to take in the rest of the day before the sun lay her red blade.

"Let's see your dives," he said.

I dove and then Cindy dove, and after he judged us both, Cindy won. No ties. She gloated silently. Her face, all smile. Not mine. My face, all scowl like my body.

"Not fair," I mumbled, sitting at the dock's edge. I dunked my feet in the water. When I looked downwards, I saw the alarming cut water makes where it meets air; my legs disjointed like eyes unable to see a faraway sight; eyes out of tandem.

"Don," said Mom in that soft tone he listened to. But then, he listened to all her tones.

"It's only a game, Rusty, for God's sake." He chuckled to make things light.

No way had Cindy beaten my Watermelon Dive. She couldn't split her legs in the air like me. Why was he making me lose? Was it because Aunt Doris beat him at swimming games? Dad never played with my feelings when we were alone, just the two of us.

There we were, driving down Grimsby's Main Street with the top down on the Malibu, the summer sun over our heads (Mom at home, fast asleep after her night shift in the ICU), doing Saturday errands. The AM radio blasting out our favourite pop songs: "Tie a Yellow Ribbon Round the Old Oak Tree" and "Love Will Keep Us Together."

Why was he making me lose? Why was I letting him be the judge of me?

I was the one Dad got mad at when Cindy left her wet bathing suit on top of the bed or when he found her damp swim towel balled on the bathroom floor. She smiled with subtle pleasure when she saw my freckled face redden.

Is that what it was like having a sister? Before Cindy came to stay with us that August, if I wanted the last Hello Dolly in the pan I got it. If I wanted to sleep in the other twin bed (my own sheets wet from night sweats), all I had to do was hop over. And when my parents sat on the dock, it was me they watched. My smooth front crawl, my perfect toe-pointed dives, my back-and-forth endurance. My skin prickled and my mouth scowled when praise went to her.

"Wanna play tubes?" Cindy asked, still treading after her win.

"No," I said, turning to Mom. "We have to eat, right?"

Mom looked at her inner wrist to see the watch face; the

old habit lived on from when she used to take patients' pulses in the ICU. "The wings won't be done yet. You have time."

But playing tubes meant standing on them for as long as possible. Another game I wasn't prepared to lose, my feelings too fierce to balance properly.

"Race you to the raft," I said in a rush. I would win this game and he couldn't stop me.

"No," said Cindy, grinning. "Think I'll float for a while." My scowl returned.

I tried to imagine Dad as a boy. "Your father was gangly like a weed," Aunt Doris said the day she dropped Cindy off for her summer stay. She told me he was good at sports, especially baseball. With those long legs of his, he could whip from base to base. But he panicked in water when he couldn't touch bottom. When I'd asked my aunt why, she told me what happened off the dock at Baie-D'Urfé where they grew up, in a house right across from the lake, how Dad and his buddy Louie were out paddling in a canoe one day when Louie stood and started rocking the boat and it tipped. Louie could swim but Dad couldn't. Somehow during his drowning panic, Dad's long arms hit the upturned canoe and he held on.

If that happened to me, I wouldn't have to hold on. I could float or tread water or swim to shore.

"NO SWIMMING TODAY, I'm afraid," Mom announced later that week. She was sitting and smoking in her chesterfield nook, her legs curled up. She was looking out the family room window at the pelting rain. "No tennis for me." She sighed.

Since our move to the quarry, she hardly played the game she loved and excelled at. As a little girl, I spent hours watching her through the diamond-link fence. *Pock!* Straight from the racquet's heart, the sweet spot, the perfect shot. My Malibu Barbie and I silently cheered.

Cindy plonked down beside me on the chesterfield. "Scoot over," she said, nudging me in the ribs. "What should we do?"

I nudged her back before waving away the annoying cigarette smoke. "Don't know," I said. I wanted to swim. I wanted the rain to stop.

Mom lit another cigarette, inhaled and exhaled. "Why don't you girls play Monopoly? The game's in the hall cupboard."

Cindy followed me—out of the family room, through the living room and down the back hall of our bungalow. At some point the sound of her soft footsteps behind me stopped. She'd slipped into the master bedroom.

"What are you doing?" I said, stepping on the plush blue carpet.

"Pictures," she said, scanning the dresser, bureau and matching bedside tables. "My parents have wedding photos… yours don't have any."

I thought back to her parents' bedroom, a room I knew well from our games of hide-and-go-seek. The window's floor-length curtain, where I hid my stilled body, smelled of ripe peach. Everything in their house smelled fresh and clean. There were wedding photos on the master bedroom wall and dresser. "So what," I said. "They eloped. They didn't have a wedding."

"Elope. Ha! Cantaloupe, antelope." She grinned and waited for me to laugh.

"You don't know, do you? You marry but not at church. A judge man does it, someone like that." *What did Mom say?*

A justice of the peace? I folded my arms across my chest. I didn't want to continue this conversation but didn't know why.

"Aunt Rusty and Uncle Don don't wear wedding rings."

I thought of Mom's bare hands. Dad's tiger-eye ring.

"Dad does."

"That's not a wedding ring." Cindy pushed back the blue sham on the king-sized bed and pulled off a pillowcase, then draped the cotton slip over the back of her head, her long brown curls. "How do I look?" She leaned against the cedar wall for a long moment before proceeding down her pretend aisle. I stepped forward. "No, stay there," she ordered. "You're the groom."

"I don't want to be the groom."

"You have to be the groom, you're taller."

She came toward me, pausing after each step, singing these words: "Here comes the bride." I hated that song. For some reason it made me think of funerals, though I'd never been to one. "Stop it. I don't want to play this stupid game."

Mom and Dad never talked about their elopement unless I pushed them, and I rarely did. The three of us were on a long car ride to Nana Florence's house in Owen Sound – it must have been just before we stopped going there. They were always extra jittery when nearing Nana's red brick house, especially during Christmastime when our stay was longer. Mom smoked even more during those long drives. Dad did too. He hadn't quit at that point. I was clouded in smoke as I lay in the back seat, drugged with Gravol to stun the motion sickness I eventually outgrew. *When did the elopement happen? Did you wear a white dress, Mom? Dad, did you wear a special suit? Didn't* somebody *take a picture?* Why was I hesitant to ask them these questions? I could feel the wall they'd built.

"Where did you elope again?" My voice was coated with sleep. They couldn't say *go play in your room*. I had them trapped. I sat up.

They glanced at each other. "Cape Cod," said Dad.

"Mom, you said Peggy's Cove."

She gave Dad a tight-eyed look. "I meant Cape Cod, honey. It's easy to get them mixed up."

Mom never made mistakes. I twisted the neck of my stuffed animal, Lambie, where I'd rubbed the fur away.

"What's with all the goddamn questions? If you knew the answer, why ask?" said Dad.

I never got any further than that. Cindy and her stupid questions, her weird fixation on my parents' wedding.

"You need to practise for the big day," said Cindy. "I'm going to have a long train, a bouquet of yellow roses and a long veil like Mom's." She sidled beside me and hooked her arm through mine. I shimmied out of her hold and elbowed her. "Oww," she said, dropping the pillowcase. "That hurt!"

"Put it back," I said, stepping over the threshold into the hallway. "I'm getting Monopoly."

WHEN THE RAIN FINALLY STOPPED, we didn't want to go swimming but wanted to be near the quarry, so we went out in the little battered rowboat. I sat in the middle and Cindy, the stern. She saw the far side of the quarry. I saw what we were leaving – the dock and the tall cottonwood trees, the cedar hedges lining our brown L-shaped bungalow, the surrounding lawn, cut weekly by Dad, and Mom's begonias and impatiens. As I rowed further a sensation trickled through me, as if I were seeing outside myself, like a flying bird or a god watching.

What did Cindy see, facing the other way? Where the bush grew thick and jungle-like and the edge of the limestone was jagged, all that green, the water a mirror soaking it up, ripe like watermelon rind. The other side, where the birds and animals lived: osprey, fox, deer.

We listened for splashes. *Fish jump!* Then we turned to the source, the dissolving water rings. When we finally made it to the other side, we looked for the great blue heron.

"Shh," I said. The bird did a good job of blending in, but when I looked closely, there she was, just like I'd told Cindy. Grey and blue and wonderful. Yellow beak and curved mesh of long grey feathers. Beady eyes and sticklike legs. She was wading on the underwater limestone ledges where I'd first sighted her, before Cindy's arrival. I rested the oars and let the boat arrow in slowly toward her.

"See?" I whispered. "Told you we'd see her."

We floated over the hazy green, the only motion the boat's soft glide; our mouths were open and speechless. And then the heron's long wings expanded, lifting her up and up, above our heads. We felt the wing-flaps of warm air.

"It's afraid," said Cindy.

"No, she's not. She knows we won't hurt her." Her airborne limbs lacked any tension, the way my limbs did when I swam underwater, away from the air-troubled world.

"You don't know that. And you don't know it's a she."

"Do so," I said. Though I couldn't recall the picture in Mom's bird book to prove my point, I had a knowing feeling.

After the heron had flown out of sight, I landed the boat on the jungle-side. We sat on one of the limestone ledges and fingered fossils I'd learned the names of in school. Snail-shaped ammonites and beetle-shaped trilobites. The question-mark curls of the nameless worms. We Brailled the language of stone.

"It's like a cemetery," Cindy said, breaking the silence. "Only the stone doesn't mark a grave, it *is* the grave. Ew!" She wiped her finger on the belly of my green bathing suit.

She was being silly and I didn't want to be silly. I wanted to keep touching the lost lives of the little. But she wouldn't stop, so I told her about the drowned woman, a story I'd overheard my parents talking about. A young woman, an orphan, had lost her will to live. The water had called to her, a mirror she could slip into to disappear, as if returning to her mother. That's not how my parents had told the story but that's how I thought of it. The image of the woman's water-cradled body. That same thrilling chill moved through me again as I told Cindy. I understood that pull.

"She tied a rope round her ankle, the other end to a rock."

"That doesn't make sense," said Cindy. "You're making that up."

I pointed to the wedge of tree and bush that led to Windmill Point Road, the road at the end of our long gravel driveway. "She lived over there."

"Alone?" said Cindy, trying to see through the greens.

I nodded.

"Who lives there now?"

I didn't answer. She was trying to change the subject to shift the disturbing image, the rock-anchored body's fall through dark watery depths.

"Her lungs would fill," I said. "And the water would bloat her."

Cindy giggled. "Sounded like you said *boat her*."

"You think it's funny? She must've been sad."

"I don't get it. Why would you want to?" She put her hand over the water's skin and flicked the surface.

"Hey!" I said, splashing her back.

We got back in the boat and I rowed us home, directly over the deepest part of the quarry. It wasn't the only spot you couldn't see rock bottom, but somehow knowing it was there gave me a crisp, eerie feeling. We were quiet when we passed over it. We knew to respect it with silence.

"Look! A hand!" I couldn't resist. I saw fear rise through my cousin's face, punching through her brown eyes. And then her eyes welled up.

"That's not funny," she said and she turned away.

That night I couldn't sleep. I watched Cindy in the twin bed beside me. Hers was the body I used to have when I was cute and small, and when her dimples popped from Dad's attention it chiselled my gut. Tucked under the covers, I stared at the room's dark and willed my body to ease and lighten, for the quarry inside me to calm again.

IT WAS MY FIRST DAY without her. I sat alone on the dock bench, the water a mirror for the limestone to fall into. Post-card pretty but all I felt was this rock-bottom ache. Even though she was thinner, and Dad said she was a better diver, I missed my cousin. I needed to learn to be alone again. I decided to go out in the boat.

I rowed through the chilly wind to the other side of the quarry and our house grew smaller and smaller. It seemed fitting that I found the lifeless body of the heron, twisted in a question-mark curl, under the leaves of the overhanging branches. It moved to the gentle waves the oars made. One wing was outstretched like a carpet. No smell of decay, as if the heron had decided to play dead like Cindy and I did between the dock and the floating raft.

I didn't think about the cause. I only wanted to fold the extended wing back in like an accordion or a fan, but I heard Cindy's voice: *it's dead, it won't know the difference.* And then this cutting feeling came with words, *leave it alone, row home.* I dunked in the oars and rowed through the quiet. The view of the jungle-side grew smaller until it blurred into one long band.

Soon it was too cold to swim, but I wanted to be inside the quarry. Mom was too tired to watch me. *I have to lie down now, dear.* When Dad finally arrived home from another sales meeting, I asked him to sit on the dock. He agreed, but once we were there I knew from the glazed look on his face that his mind was elsewhere.

"Dad," I said, blocking his line of vision. "Aren't you watching?" I waved my arms.

"I'm watching."

I dove in.

"Nice About-to-Die Dive," he said as I climbed up the ladder.

"Thanks." I slicked back my hair and readied myself for the next one.

"Nice Drowning Dive," he said. His praise trickled through my dripping body. I wanted more.

"I'm going in again, Dad. Ready?"

"Ready."

"Nice," he said when I climbed back up.

This time I didn't feel the trickle of praise running through me. With nobody to be nice against, his "nice" meant nothing.

IT WAS THE DAY BEFORE Christmas Eve and I was sitting in the family room on the curve of the chesterfield, watching a horse-drawn covered wagon trundle across the television screen, when the phone call in the kitchen reached its peak. Mom was talking to Aunt Doris. The Brants were coming to our house this Christmas holiday. I couldn't wait.

"Maybe you'll come to my funeral then," Mom said into the telephone, her voice high-pitched, a tone foreign to my ears.

I shifted from my curled-up position, ready to jump.

Dad lunged into the kitchen from his office and grabbed the receiver. "Doris! That's enough! How dare you make Rusty cry." He slammed down the phone.

My funeral. After Mom said those words, I knew what was hidden inside that horse-drawn covered wagon—a closed coffin, and inside the coffin, my mother.

I felt strangely removed from the scene in the yellow kitchen, just as I felt strangely removed from the new wig on Mom's head and her puffy cheeks. Mom was crying and she never cried. I'd been witness to this family fallout between Mom and Dad and Dad's younger sister Doris, and I wished I hadn't. I was in their line of vision but they weren't looking at me. Dad's arm around the slope of Mom's shaking shoulders. Her tiny sobs. She was working hard to hold them in. Something she knew how to do, hold things in. But they didn't see me watching them. It was as if I wasn't there.

"What happened?" I said, stepping into the kitchen. "Aren't they coming for Christmas?" My stomach knotted.

The snow had started up again and the evening wind was whipping it against the kitchen window, a chipping sound like chattering teeth.

"Fine," Dad said. "We'll have Christmas without them. Caitlin, you hear that?" He let go of Mom's shoulders and looked out the window. "A little snow... some excuse. *Storm?* I'll show them *storm*. She never worries when I'm driving, right, Russ? One-way road, I tell you. It's always been that way. She can hurt me all she wants but not you." He stared out at the white-flaking dark.

I was shocked. Christmas without my aunt and uncle, my cousins. The two older boys I wouldn't miss, but Cindy? "Cindy's not coming? What about our gifts?" No homemade dolls or hard-sucking sweets or hard-backed Nancy Drews. Nobody to show my presents to.

Didn't they know Mom was sick? Though Dad said she was getting better. The drugs that made her hair fall out and rounded her face were good things, temporary side effects. Mom was getting better. That's what Dad said.

I thought back to that day, in early October. The bungalow was quiet when I got home from school. Both cars parked in the carport, so the quiet didn't make sense. I should be hearing Dad's voice. He should be talking to Mom about his day. I looked out the kitchen window at the quarry. White-caps up and gone in an instant.

"Hello?"

No answer. I walked through the kitchen into the family room, and when I got there, I stopped.

There was Dad in the Windsor chair, hands on his forehead, leaning forward, and there was Mom, curled in her chesterfield nook, the ashtray heaped with pink-rimmed butts. Was it the *Merck Manual* lying there, was that my clue? The leather-bound book from her nursing school days, tucked in the curve of her legs?

23

"We have something to tell you," Dad said, staring at the floor.

I clutched my binder to my chest. And then these words flew out of my mouth: "It's cancer, isn't it?"

He didn't look up.

Mom turned to me. "I'm sorry," she said, butting out her cigarette. "I didn't want this to happen to you."

It didn't happen to me, Mom. It happened to you.

I watched the layers of smoke float through the room.

How could the Brant family not come?

Under the dock light, through the hurtling snow, the quarry waved metallic grey, the steel grey of machinery. No skin had formed yet, so snow absorbed into it, a seasoned cauldron of cold soup.

I didn't want cold winter. I wanted it to be warm like summer when Cindy was here. The long months of waiting for her return would have no payoff now. Had Cindy heard the phone call from her end? Was she upset about us not being together for Christmas? A chill ran down my spine, an icy mouse.

I returned to the chesterfield to watch TV. The snow had stopped making that chipping sound, but the night wind howled.

Dad offered me his glass of milk, his nightly ritual to help him fall asleep. "Have some. It'll help tonight."

I didn't want the milk, but the charged atmosphere remained, so I took a sip.

"Good girl," he said, taking back the glass.

"Sleep well, honey," said Mom. Her shoulders were calm but her voice held sadness in it. Outside the family room window, the shadowy tube of the bird feeder swung back and forth, the winter birds hidden in bushes and trees. "We'll have our own family Christmas," said Mom. "Just the three of us."

CHRISTMAS MORNING I AWOKE to a quiet house. I picked up the box of worry dolls sitting on my bedside table, last year's Christmas gift from Aunt Doris. "Just for you," she'd said. When I lifted off the oval lid of the tiny bamboo box, six wiry dolls in bright colours were clumped inside it. "They're called worry dolls," said Aunt Doris. "All the way from Guatemala. For my little worrier." She smiled.

I'd set out all six last night. I told each doll the same worries: *I wish the Brant family was here for Christmas. I wish Mom's cancer would go away.* But then I realized, those weren't worries, they were wishes.

I dropped the dolls back in the box and pushed down the lid. I felt the worries inside my stomach – expanding, contracting.

I thought Mom and Dad were still asleep when I got up, the house was so quiet, but they were sitting in the family room drinking their morning coffee. I walked through the layers of smoke and sat down on the chesterfield. "Can we open our presents now?"

They nodded.

We moved to the living room, beside the small twinkling tree, and opened up gifts. I got what I wanted – the new record *Donny & Marie: Featuring Songs from Their Television Show.* But no homemade dolls or homemade sweets or hardbacked Nancy Drews. Nobody to show my presents to.

The sky shone extra bright outside. Clear and blue, no hint of storm. Not even a breeze. The predicted snow hadn't come, so a nervous winter driver like Aunt Doris would have been fine on the busy highway, taking her time. She'd have been fine driving Uncle Jim's station wagon—his one arm in a sling from his squash accident, the two boys teasing their little brown-eyed sister in the back seat—but that phone call had piled a snow bank so high, nobody could pass through it.

The Pink-Shingled Cottage

BEFORE MY PARENTS BOUGHT the house by the quarry
we spent summer holidays in Southampton. The compact
interior of the pink-shingled cottage smelled of Lake Huron
water and Lake Huron sand plus the nearby cedar and pine
trees. These outdoor scents mingled tightly with indoor
scents: QT tanning lotion, The Dry Look hairspray, Old Spice,
Benson & Hedges, Chanel No 5.

Everyday Mom played the sport she loved at the nearby
tennis club. With a backhand as strong as her forehand,
she could whack any oncoming ball. Singles. Doubles. She
played to win, dressed in her home-made Simplicity-pattern
tennis dresses. Spectators loved to watch her skillful playing.
But of all the eyes watching, none shone like those of her
biggest fan.

Rusty, always my champion.

These were the words Dad had engraved on a silver ID bracelet after she lost a close match. She didn't like to be defeated. Dad thought the gift would cheer her up, and it did.

One day she left the bracelet sitting by the cottage kitchen sink. I fastened it to my wrist but it rolled right off. *You'll never be a champion,* said the voice in my head.

There was a rich American who admired my mother's talent for tennis, and he often asked her to play. Mom always beat Mr. Davy, but he worked hard to narrow the gap. His tanned face trickled with sideburns and his silver hair, slick with dark streaks. He and his non-playing wife would drop by the pink-shingled cottage after round robins. Mrs. Davy always wore her hair pulled back in an elegant bun (Mom called it a chignon). Her complexion was clear and tanned. It didn't freckle out of control like Mom's summer face.

Rye and ginger. Rum and Coke. I helped Dad bartend. One evening he was telling a joke in his fake Québécois accent, the ladies listening intently from across the kitchen table. He was getting closer to the punchline. I could hear the rising rhythm. Mr. Davy looked bored standing by the screen door.

"Here you go," I said, handing him his rum and Coke.

The ice tinkled when he shook the glass. "You don't play, do you?" he said. "But you've got a racquet."

I nodded.

He looked me up and down. "Your mother is an amazing player. I'd be surprised if you didn't have some of that in you." He took a sip and watched me. His Adam's apple flickered up.

It would be rude to turn away. He smacked his lips. *My signal to go?*

"Bet you see three rolls of fat when you're sitting in the tub," he whispered. He stared at my stomach, where the worry lived. "Am I right, Caitlin?"

"Three," I said, not knowing what else to say.

"Hey," said Dad. His voice rose above the ladies' laughter. "Where's my little bartender?"

"Go," said Mr. Davy, winking.

That night when Mom came into my room to kiss me goodnight, I asked her if she thought I was fat.

"You're not fat."

I pushed back the blanket and lifted my gingham nightie, grabbed a chunk of flesh. "What's this then?" I said, eyeing her.

She smiled. "It's puppy fat, honey. I had it too when I was ten. Not to worry, you'll grow out of it."

I thought of the silver ID bracelet that didn't fit. I thought of the tennis balls I couldn't hit.

Red Bars

I SAT IN THE BACK SEAT OF Mom's Malibu convertible, fingering the seat-belt buckle, half-listening to Mom and her new friend Eleanor, a long-time member of the church we'd started going to after our first Christmas at the quarry. I was going for my Bronze Medallion and I needed a new bathing suit. My green Speedo left indents on my shoulders. Red bars.

It was the beginning of March break, and we were taking the back route, the safe route, to the mall, instead of the highway, so Mom wouldn't make those sharp intakes of breath (no transport trucks to pass us). Mom, like Aunt Doris, disliked highway driving. But we didn't talk about Aunt Doris like we didn't talk about Cindy and her time at the quarry. Despite having avoided the highway, Mom seemed high-strung, her mouth tight as she nodded in response to Eleanor's yammering.

"Did you see when she pushed up her sleeve? She must've forgotten they were there, until she saw me looking from down the pew." Eleanor shook her head. "I don't know how Carol can stay with him."

"It's not so easy to leave a husband," said Mom.

"Come on, if Don started doing that? Henry, if he so much as gives me the evil eye, I'm at him with my broom." Eleanor laughed.

Mom, squeezing the wheel hard with both hands, was oblivious to my watching her. I stared at the squiggles congregating on her nose, red like her wig. She never found her original shade, so a deeper auburn had to do. It fell flat on her head like a bathing cap. Not like her real hair, those subtle waves. So different from Eleanor's coarse black spikes.

That first time she went to the hospital, no one told me she had cancer. "Your mother's going to have a woman's operation." I wore barrettes then, and I remember touching the cold metal after Dad said those words. The barrettes had red birds painted on them. If you looked close enough, you could see music notes seeping from their beaks.

Woman's operation.

We lived in Grimsby. No quarry yet. Our flat-roofed house was built next to the beauty of the Niagara Escarpment. Upside-Down House. Bedrooms downstairs. Kitchen and living room up. "Weird," said the kids I played with. "Your house is weird. Your own bathroom?" They said it like I had a disease. I stopped inviting them over.

I should've known better about the birds. But once they were clipped in, I forgot about them, like the way you forget you've got ice cream on your chin, until someone points.

We were standing in line, in the school hallway. The scent of lemon drifted from the janitor's floor polisher moving down the hall. I was thinking about the "woman's operation." What did that mean? Would I need one when I grew up? Why hadn't Mom told me?

"You're in my way," said Gail, the classmate standing behind me.

We'd been put into alphabetical order. Otherwise, I'd never stand in front of Gail. She nudged my waist with the cut of her elbow. I turned toward her, my body's response.

"Birds," she said, her voice, a sharp tweak. "Little birdies singing music notes. Isn't that cute?" When she snickered, her shoulders hunched. She turned to the girl behind her. "See how red she went this time?" Gail whispered. "Check her out."

I could never tell the little birds apart. Chickadees and juncos were both small and bouncy and mostly grey. Mom said I needed to pay closer attention, to spend more time seeing what was there, right in front of me. Her favourite was the cardinal. Not the male with his bright red, showy feathers but the subdued female, her feathers a warm, red-tinged brown.

Sometimes while playing outside, I found a feather lying on the ground. I would pick it up and bring it back to Mom. She collected them in a vase by the windowsill. Blooms of feathery light.

The line began to move. Mrs. Styles, our music teacher, welcomed us at the door to her classroom. "*Fiddler on the Roof*! 'Sunrise, Sunset'! Hope you know your lyrics!"

I headed to the back and opened *Songbook Five*, held it like a wall.

AT SEARS WE MANAGED TO AVOID the spray-attacks of the perfume ladies. Eleanor wasn't interested and Mom already had her scent: Chanel No. 5. We were picking our way through the bathing-suit section when Mom suddenly veered us away. I hid the glossy black one piece that I wanted on a shelf—the tight fabric would help flatten my stomach – and wedged myself through the clacking of racks.

"What do you think?" Mom smiled as she held up a white cotton nightgown.

The neckline was bordered with baby-blue cross-stitching, a simple yet intricate pattern. It made me think of ants, their bodies snipped and glued into complex shapes.

"Here. This goes with it," Eleanor said, holding the matching robe. She pressed a long sleeve into my hand.

The fabric was so bright, I thought the black bathing suit, the last thing I'd touched, would leave a mark.

"Will it be warm enough?" I said, touching the robe. "You get cold at night, Mom." Even post-treatment, Mom still got the chills.

"Not for Rusty," Eleanor said, "for you."

Mom passed Eleanor the nightgown, and Eleanor held it up to my chest for Mom to see. After they nodded, I was told to look in the mirror.

The straps were the width of bathing-suit straps and the bodice was lined with piping a shade lighter than the blue of the intricate pattern. I couldn't help but think, *isn't this what women wear on their wedding night? Women with breasts?*

"I don't get it," I said and looked at Mom in the oval mirror. She was looking at my chest. Her eyes wide and watery, as if she were filling in the gaps.

I went home that day with an expensive nightgown set,

not the black Speedo I wanted. So I crossed my arms as Mom drove us home. I lowered my head and sulked.

THE DAY OF MY Bronze Medallion exam, I barely fit into my old green Speedo. Elastic cut into all parts it touched.

I pushed the red bars out of my mind and I did what the examiner told me to do: I swam the full length of the Centennial Pool underwater. I breathed my Tic Tac breath into the sour-smelling mouth of a bony boy. I saved two pseudo-drowners. All the while Mom, like the other moms, watched through the glass.

After the last rescue, the examiner huddled us into a corner. One by one, she called out the names of the students who had passed. When she finished, we all stood up. We had to walk by the glass window to get back to the change room, and because I was last in the line of six, I witnessed all the thumbs-up and hand waves the students gave to their mothers. The hand waves the mothers gave back were even more manic. When I saw red from the corner of my eye, I knew Mom was watching me. *So?*

I looked the other way.

A few weeks later, when the badge arrived in the mail, Mom congratulated me. By then she knew I'd passed, but I hadn't told her when she needed me to, standing there with the healthy mothers, waiting.

"You mean you passed?" She'd said this to me in the car after I told her on the drive home. She tightened her grip on the wheel. "Why did you wait to tell me? Why?" Her voice had no anger in it.

I pressed my middle finger against the buckle that strapped me in and watched it turn red.

"Look!" I said, and pulled down the neck of my sweater. From the expression on Mom's face, I knew the red bar wasn't there.

Perhaps that's why, when she handed me the badge, I went straight to my room and threw it in the closet. Why I lay on my bed and turned on the clock radio to muffle my crying.

Lifeguard

THE SWIMMING POOL at Hideaway Park Campground was empty except for a chubby girl in the shallow end, pushing a flutter board, and a gangly boy in the deep end, cannon-balling. They were no trouble to watch, and they knew how to swim. But then Sean and his taller buddy walked in through the chain-link gate and started pushing each other toward the edge of the pool.

I got up from my seat by the diving board and slowly walked toward them. I could feel my heart beating fast. I held the string of my silver whistle like a leash leading the way.

"No horsing around," I said and pointed to the sign: *Rules of the Pool*. But with the chipped paint it read: *Rules the Pool*.

They stopped and pulled their arms away from each other as if opening a human lock. "No horsing around," I said to fill the silence. I pushed back my sun visor. "Okay?"

Sean grinned and his little teeth showed. He was the son of the married couple who owned the campground, the people I worked for the summer before my last year of high school. I was seventeen. I'd already spent two summers slicing and wrapping deli meat at Simon's Super Save. Lifeguarding was better. Not so nerdy and it paid more money. I was saving up for university, though I still didn't know what I wanted to be. "Be a lawyer," Dad said. "You like to read. You're always reading. Don't let someone be the boss of you. You be the boss. I had smarts like you, you know, but I couldn't do school. You can do school, just like your mother."

Sean looked like he was about to say something when his taller, blonder friend said, "Is that your name?" He pointed to my T-shirt.

"Yes," I said, and laughed. "My name is Life. Life Guard."

"Nice to meet you, Life Guard." He put out his hand. It was warm and smooth, not moist or sticky. "I'm Darren," he said. "And you know Sean. Nice to meet you, Life."

THE NEXT DAY I saw him through the pool's chain-link fence, across the long mown field, hanging around with Sean and some other boys in the Games Room. The Games Room was like a garage, and with the door open you could see straight in. They popped coins into the Pac-Man and pinball machines. I heard the whiz and whir throughout my shift. I saw wild lights flashing.

Later I saw him leaning against the Games Room wall.

I knew he was watching me. My right hand curled toward the memory of his hand touching mine.

While locking up the pool's gate at the end of my shift, I heard his voice, his American twang.

"Life."

I turned.

"I left my watch in there." He pointed to the far corner.

"You think so?" I said, and reopened the metal lock.

The gate creaked when he pushed through it. He headed straight for the corner he'd pointed to. I should've checked his wrist. Was he having a go at me? But I was too busy fixing the sun-dried wisps poking out from beneath my visor.

"There," he said. He gave the watch a shake and fastened it over the white strip on his wrist. "Thanks, Caitlin." Our arms brushed when he passed me.

"You know my name," I said without thinking.

He turned to the Games Room, to his waiting friends. "Bunch of us are having a keg party at the back field tonight. You should come." He walked across the coarse grass and stopped. "Okay?" he said, looking back.

Dad's Caddy wasn't there when I pulled Mom's Malibu into the carport. Another night he was late coming home, his pattern since Nana's arrival to help with Mom's home care. Nana was back in our lives again after what seemed like a long gap. Before I headed into the bungalow, I looked to the quarry. The wind quivered the water and the sun bled its gold band. Then I saw Mom and Nana sitting outside. They were drinking lemonade, the fizzy kind that Eleanor made. Pink like Mom's pinkest lipstick. When Mom sipped the drink it made her lips shine. When Nana sipped it, her lips stayed brick red. Red like her house in Owen Sound, the house Mom grew up in, a two-storey brick house sitting empty, waiting for Nana to move back in.

"It's only temporary," Mom had said to Dad when the pain became too much, an invisible entity that wouldn't go away, that took more of her each year we lived by the quarry. But it wasn't temporary. When Nana came, Nana stayed.

Her eyes stared us down before her next biting comment. The three of us were on edge, fearful of her wrath. She'd softened a bit while living with us. Mom's illness had done that, I supposed. A good thing for Mom, but Nana just transferred that pointed energy at me and Dad, especially Dad. So there was always tension in the house, hovering like the cigarette smoke Nana hated. One dislike we had in common.

Nana never missed an opportunity to nitpick. One evening, as we sat at the gate-leg table in the family room after our meal, she watched in disgust as Dad spread generous layers of butter, then peanut butter, over slices of white bread "How do you have room for *that* after your dinner?" Loud smacking noises came from his mouth, a grin on his face. When Nana wasn't looking, he winked at me. She sipped her hot water and milk and shook her head.

"Caitlin," Dad said one night. "It's time you did the dishes."

"Why don't *you* do them?"

"Honey," said Mom, returning to her chesterfield nook. "There aren't many. It won't take long."

Another night, after our meal, Dad grabbed hold of the empty bread bag and its plastic tab. "Here, Caitlin. Throw these out."

"Wait," said Nana. "Give me that."

He paused before passing her the bread tab.

"Waste not, want not," she said, tucking it in her pantsuit

jacket. She would add it to the growing stack on the kitchen windowsill. Bread tabs, elastic bands, twist-ties. "What the hell are we keeping them for?" Dad asked Mom when Nana left the family room. "Does she think it's the Great Depression?"

"Just go along with it, Don. She means no harm. It's just her way."

Mom put down her lemonade and smiled when I approached. Nana looked up from her knitting but didn't smile. She was waiting for me to slip up. Those blue saucer eyes – I felt them on me even when she wasn't in the room.

It was good to see Mom out of bed. This meant she was having a good day. Despite the early July heat, she had that awful orange-and-brown afghan draped over her lap, one of the many things around the house Nana had made. "From duty, not love," Dad often said.

"Save any lives today?" Mom asked.

I couldn't see her eyes. She was wearing those sunglasses, ugly bug-eyed goggles that blocked the light, damage done by chemicals that did terrible things to save her body.

"Three. Including mine. What's for dinner?" I said, not waiting for an answer. "I'm going out later. I can grab something quick."

"I've made your favourite," said Nana firmly. "Five-in-One."

It wasn't my favourite anymore and hadn't been for years. Rice and ground beef and chopped onion and celery, casseroled in a can of tomato soup, a red soupy mess. At least it was better than Dad's one-trick supper: wieners and beans.

Before Nana's arrival, when it was just the three of us, we were sitting at the gate-leg table eating wieners and beans.

Dad's shoulders were swaying to the jazzy theme song from the CBC radio show *As It Happens*. He loved listening to the interviews from around the world. Sometimes I wondered if he wished he were conducting them. Dad had a voice people listened to.

"You're doing great, Russ," Dad said.

Mom was halfway through her dinner.

A moment later she dropped her fork and clutched her drug-riddled stomach. "Don, the bag."

He grabbed hold of the plastic bag and held it open like a mouth.

My stomach curdled to her guttural heaves, the chew-chunk smells filling the family room. "Gross," I said without thinking, without realizing what I was saying.

Mom took hold of the bag and continued to heave.

Dad glared at me. "Gross?" He reached for the radio knob. Barbara Frum's voice disappeared. "You think that's *gross?*"

I wanted to take back my words but it was too late. "Yes," I said, pushing back my half-eaten meal. "I can't eat this."

Mom stopped heaving. "Hand me a Kleenex, Don," she said. She wiped her eyes and lips.

I looked at the brown pool of beans on my plate and cradled my queasy stomach.

"Go to your room," he said, "or I'll show you *gross*."

I got up from my chair without looking at them and went straight through my bedroom to the adjoining bathroom, where my face filled the medicine-cabinet mirror like a bloated balloon. *I'll show you gross*, it said. I pulled up my blouse and grabbed the chunky flesh between my ribs and waist.

It was Mom who came to my room that night to see how

I was doing. After knocking at my door, she sat at the edge of my bed. I dog-eared my novel for English class, *The Stone Angel*, and set it on my lap. *Is Nana like Hagar Shipley underneath that stony exterior?* There was talk of Nana coming to stay with us "to help out." I tried to imagine a softer side to her but couldn't.

The colour had returned to Mom's face. "Your show's on in a couple of minutes," she said. It was the sequel to the episode we'd watched together last week: Mary Ingalls going blind. "Your father says he'll watch the ball game in the bedroom." She squeezed my calf and stood up. "Come on, honey."

"I didn't mean—"

"I know," she said, and left the room.

I reopened my book. "*I know, I know. How long have I known? Or have I always known, in some far crevice of my heart, some cave too deeply buried, too concealed?*"

The wind hit my face. I looked at Mom's wheelchair. She couldn't do that anymore—walk to my room, see if I was okay.

Nana checked her gold watch. It shone like her one gold tooth. She touched her hearing aid and said, "Six o'clock and he's still not home. I hope he likes a cold dinner."

"I have time for a swim then?" I looked at Mom. I already knew Nana's answer.

"A quick one, dear. Mother, will you wheel me to the dock?"

I dove right in. I didn't toe-test the water as usual. I swam underwater as far as I could, until I couldn't hold my breath anymore. I still couldn't reach the floating raft, but I was getting closer each time. I front-crawled the gap and clung to a metal barrel. How is it that something so heavy on land floats on water? I'd taken physics but couldn't understand it. I memorized the equations and plopped them in. Didn't know what they meant or how to work through them, only knew by intuition. When Mr. Justice handed back our tests, I saw a happy face stamped beside my grade. *You can't fake physics.* Somehow, I could.

The barrel was slimy underneath with a dark green, slippery crust. Algae, I guessed. Like the green on the bottom rungs of the wooden raft's ladder, the submerged ones.

A body at rest stays at rest, locked inside a wheelchair. But she could still use a walker; she still had good days. Mom had been sick so long now it was hard to remember her as healthy. Another tug in the nugget of my belly. A daughter can suck out mother energy, even through air. Day by day, her healthy body had seeped into mine. I was the sun-drenched barrel above the quarry's surface; Mom, the guck-ridden part.

When I glanced back at the dock, I saw two women looking out at a seventeen-year-old girl hanging on to a metal barrel, her body strong from daily swims, her black Speedo clinging to her never-thin-enough torso.

"WHERE DID YOU SAY you were going?" Dad stood beside the gate-leg table, next to the place not set for him, and dropped his red silk tie there. Nana's blue eyes glared at him — *pick it up.*

"Back to Hideaway Park," I said, gently tossing his tie onto the chesterfield. "With Brenda."

He bit his bottom lip and unbuttoned his dress shirt, revealing dark curls in the V of his chest. He scanned my empty plate, lined with the remnants of Nana's Five-in-One, and smiled when he saw Mom's empty plate. "What's so good?" He smacked his lips.

I was safe then. I put down my knife and fork. Nana eyed my haphazard placement.

I edged the cutlery to its proper place.

I DECIDED TO KEEP the top up on the Malibu even though Brenda wanted it down. I didn't want my hair blowing all over. Dad never had that problem when he drove Mom's convertible. With so much The Dry Look hairspray on his hair, it was as stiff as a Ken doll's. Brenda blew her cigarette smoke out the passenger window, but I could smell it clouding my skin. It had a weedier smell than Mom's Benson & Hedges. Brenda tucked the box of Player's back into her purse.

Brenda didn't go to my high school. She took a bus in the opposite direction. Fort Erie Secondary, a school where less was expected from students. Who needs Grade thirteen when there are good-paying jobs at local factories, with regular paycheques, a place to go. Say goodbye to more tests and boring teachers, the strict confines of institutional brick. With university in my near future, factory life would not happen to me. Dad was right. School was something I could do, always on the Honour Roll. Why question this?

During the school year, whenever I made my way over the railway tracks, the little hill on Windmill Point Road where the killdeer nested, I saw Brenda waiting for her bus. There was never a knapsack on her shoulders or any books in her hands. She was a huddle in the distance, a huddle that boarded a bus.

One mid-June day her school bus was late. We waited in silence on opposite sides of Dominion Road. She looked one way. Me, the other.

"Want one?" she said, crossing the empty street. She unsealed a fresh pack of Player's. The cellophane blew in the gust of wind.

"I don't smoke."

"You should," she said. She smiled. She had a gap between her front teeth big enough to squeeze the side of her tongue through. My gap was too thin for that.

"Bad habit," she said, giving the cigarette a bug-eyed look. "Cancer stick but it keeps me sane.

I cringed at her use of that word, but she didn't notice. She was cupping her mouth with one hand and flicking her lighter with the other. The flame wouldn't hold. She turned to block the wind.

"I'm Brenda," she said, turning to face me. Smoke weaved between us. "You live across from us, at that quarry, eh? It's Caitlin, right?"

"I think your bus is coming, Brenda."

"Shit." She dropped her cigarette on the gravel and squished it with her shoe, a running shoe, a generic brand.

"You like Tom Petty?" she said, crossing back.

"Yeah."

"I have his latest, *Hard Promises*. Come over after school. We'll listen to it."

The bus groaned to a stop and Brenda stepped on. She headed to the back. When my bus arrived two minutes later, I sat near the front.

HER HOUSE, a rundown farmhouse with dust bunnies the size of birds' nests and cat hair clumps on the cushions (Nana would be horrified), gave me an escape. I could avoid Mom's sickness, Nana's watchful eyes, and Dad's bad moods.

I revelled in the disarray of the dirty dishes, the unmade beds, the cup-ring stains on the side tables, even the musty smell of cat dander, away from the sting of Nana's cleaning ammonia.

Brenda wasn't a stoner or a headbanger, but I knew from the peach tightness of her jeans, the way her thighs rubbed together when she walked, her broad forehead and eyes caked with black eyeliner that congealed in the corners, if she went to Ridgeway High I wouldn't talk to her. Not that I had a reputation to uphold or anything. Quiet girl, shy girl, cat-got-your-tongue-and-chewed-it-up-like-pink-gum girl, I walked the halls with downcast eyes. I bristled to the itch of girls' giggles.

At least I wasn't a nerdy girl, like those girls who wore odd-coloured sweaters – pea greens, banana yellows. They didn't know how to be invisible. They were so out there with their oddball ways. Bad perms and tacky-coloured lipstick. They were walking targets for the mouthy girls. The ones too clumsy to be cheerleaders and not pretty enough to stun the boys, but smart enough to know the only way to survive the endless days of high-school boredom was to power your way through it.

Nobody witnessed my friendship with Brenda. I was safe driving down Dominion, breathing in her second-hand smoke, driving us to Hideaway Park.

THE KEG PARTY was at the back of the campground, away from trailers and tents. We stood around the picnic table as if it were the focus of something. The middle-of-the-night theft had been a group effort: Sean, Bulldog, JP, Darren. They'd painstakingly rolled the keg from its starting point at Cherry Hill Golf Club, a good mile from here, all the way down Garrison Road, and then hidden it in the backwoods so Chuck the groundskeeper wouldn't find it. They couldn't stop talking about their heroic efforts. Brenda and I stood listening.

"When do we get some?" asked Brenda.

"Here," said Bulldog, passing me his plastic cup.

The beer was flat and warm. I drank it anyway.

I jumped when Sean said, "Shit! Truck! Grab your stuff!"

We ran into the woods and listened for the sound of tires rolling over gravel. Chuck flashed the Ford's high beams but not in our direction. It was hard to see in the dark, and the branches kept poking me.

"I left my cigs on the picnic table," said Brenda, moving forward.

Sean pulled her back. "Hell, he's not interested in your Player's. Keep down, he's doing a U-ey."

Someone grabbed my hand and pulled me from the group. I knew from the fit whose hand it was.

"He's gone," announced Bulldog. "Coast's clear." Of all the boys, Bulldog had the sharpest accent. Cheektowaga, Tonawanda, one of the wandas. Darren was from Buffalo. Their parents had trailers here. They'd been coming to Hideaway Park for years.

Darren squeezed my hand. "Stay," he whispered.

A sound like peeing in a plastic cup.

"Stop hogging the beer, JP," said Bulldog.

"Piss off," said JP.

We crouched down and watched their silhouettes resume positions around the picnic table. I felt voyeuristic watching them, wrapped in the scents of cedar and pine and Darren. We were the only ones in the woods now.

48

"Where's Caitlin?" said Brenda. She was lighting a cigarette. "And where's Darren?"

"Shh," said Darren, his breath on my neck. The yellow bandana around his head smelled of sun-dried cotton.

"She's looking for me," I whispered.

He leaned back. "Okay, then."

We rose from our crouched positions and Darren led the way. As we weaved through the branches, he kept hold of my hand.

"There they are," said Brenda. The group turned.

It was then I let go of his hand. I wanted to hold it, but only when we were alone.

THE NEXT DAY, while walking around the pool, I saw Darren standing outside the Games Room. His lean body was angled toward me, his yellow bandana wrapped around his head. I knew he could see me, my fingers tingled. So I put my arm up, high in the air, and waved it like the metronome on Mom's piano, the upright grand she never played anymore. She used to play it at parties when we lived at the Upside-Down House.

He likes me, I can do this.

He stepped inside the Games Room without waving back.

I moved away from the chain-link fence. Had anyone seen me? One of the sunbathing mothers tucked her head under her fat paperback. Two girls in the shallow end giggled. I grabbed hold of my whistle and checked the perimeter of the pool.

I recalled the first time I'd been told somebody liked me. We'd just moved to the quarry. Bertie Senior School. Head scarves were in style that fall, or so I thought. I knew nobody. Nobody knew me. But soon they did, thanks to my blue paisley head scarf. Before Mr. Tribe, our homeroom teacher, sauntered in, a boy from the back pulled the head scarf down. Everyone laughed. I pulled it back up. I wasn't thinking. He was so quiet in his approach, I didn't hear him coming up behind me again.

"Do you want to know who likes you?" said Jenny Colucci, the loudest nerd in homeroom. The secret about to burst from between her buckteeth.

We were standing in the hallway waiting for the bell to ring. Even though I no longer wore the scarf (the "flicker" had moved on to fresh targets), I avoided homeroom until Mr. Tribe's arrival.

I shook my head. I was surprised at my answer. It was as if my head had a voice separate from my mouth.

"Oh," said Jenny, her fat lips curling. But she had to tell me.

That day I learned that a boy who humiliated you could be the boy who liked you.

It hadn't occurred to me that what I'd done last night in the woods had signalled to Darren: *I don't like you.* Not until now.

"Darren said something about you not holding his hand," Bulldog said when he dropped by the pool that afternoon. "I told him—get over it. You like him, right?" Bulldog was the youngest of the Hideaway boys. He was also the biggest. Squinty eyes, extended jaw. He liked to look at your mouth to see if you were listening.

I blushed.

"Thought so."

"Brenda likes you."

"Yeah, they always do." He turned to the shimmering pool. "Those girls."

When we all gathered that night, Darren took hold of my hand. I let him take it and I didn't let go.

The following day he gave me a stone he'd painted brown, with the date of our first kiss in yellow – the moment we became a true couple. When it wasn't in my palm reviving the tingle, it was on top of the towel in my Adidas bag. The colours matched the paint on the pool sign. No more *Rules the Pool*. The word "of" restored by my first boyfriend.

THEY WERE BORED NOW that the keg they'd stolen from Cherry Hill Golf Club was empty, the silver carcass found by Chuck. *He doesn't have proof. He doesn't know it was us.* They all said this. But I knew Chuck knew by that look in his eye, that high-beam gaze.

Pac-Man and pinball were no substitution. Darren spent less time in the Games Room, more time in the back field where the keg used to be. I didn't see him through the pool's chain-link fence anymore. The stone in my hand, my only comfort.

"What do you guys do back there?" He was walking me to the Malibu like he always did after the end of my shift, but I couldn't see his face. The plan was for me to come back later with Brenda. "Why are you walking so fast?"

He stopped. And when he turned, the late sunlight hit him; his eyes were glazed with red squiggles.

"Why are your eyes so red?"

He laughed, and when he tilted his neck, I could see how thick the glaze was.

"It's not right," I said. I thought of the druggies at school, their long scraggly hair and rocker T-shirts. Skipping school. Failing tests. Losers.

"What do *you* know?" His eyes narrowed. "Ever tried it?"

I froze.

"Caitlin," he said. "If you don't want me to, I'll stop."

His eyes softened. Too soft, liquid rushing down a drain.

"Don't you wanna know what I got ya?" He pulled a necklace from his pocket—an arrow on a silver chain—and swung it back and forth.

I stared at the swaying arrow. "Are you trying to hypnotize me?"

"Here. It's special." He clasped it around my neck. "Like you."

Cold on the hollow of my throat.

I WANTED TO TELL Brenda what had happened, but she wouldn't stop talking on the drive back to the campground. Bulldog this. Bulldog that. "Do you think he'll be there?" she asked.

"Yeah, he'll be there. Why wouldn't he be there? He's always there. Like JP, Sean and Darren." There. I got to say the name I wanted.

"JP's cute though, eh? Don't you think? In a skinny rocker kinda way?"

We found them in the back field beside the woods, sipping Moody Blue by the picnic table. They had almost finished the first bottle when they passed the second to us.

"Oops," said Brenda, after a gassy burp. When she looked my way, we giggled. Bulldog kept watching my mouth.

"Dribble," he said, and wiped it.

Brenda squirmed and looked away.

They'd necked. They'd done more than neck.

"Did it hurt?" The last time we lay on Brenda's canopied

bed I'd asked her this. Her bed wasn't the Sears model, the one that I wanted. Hers was handmade. Built by Brenda's second stepfather, a burly man she called "Nick." Nick smelled like the stain of the canopied wood when he didn't smell like stale beer.

"No," she said, crossing her legs. "Well, yes," she said, re-opening them.

When Bulldog wiped the drop from the other side of my mouth, Brenda stopped squirming. "You guys should see Caitlin's quarry," she said, avoiding my eyes.

This time I squirmed.

She told them it was a mini-lake stocked with fish – perch, catfish, bass – and that the limestone made the water so soft, it was like swimming in hair conditioner. "Like Timotei, feel," she said, and nudged JP. He fingered her feathered bangs. They were long like his.

"Yeah," he said. "Nice."

She let his touch linger there. We all watched except Bulldog, who grabbed for the Moody Blue. After downing another swig, he burped bully loud. JP dropped his hand. Bulldog looked at Brenda's mouth.

"The limestone's in Buffalo, right?" she said, ignoring his burp.

"Buffalo breakwater," I said. "You can see the line of limestone along the water's edge when you cross the Peace Bridge."

I thought of the black-and-white photos hanging on the family room wall, the excavation in progress, the quarrymen working the pit of the open mine from 1895 to 1903. The slabs of limestone cut like cake slices. Workhorses pulling the goods. Wooden wagons along wooden tracks. No water then – a giant tub, empty.

I imagined it happening. *Upon ignition, the dynamite stuffed carefully inside the metal pipes triggers the groundwater, the buried spring. The dormant water rises like a running bath. Did the men get out in time? The horses?* Years later, local scuba divers reported some equipment was still down there, a quarryman's graveyard in our backyard, an aquarium of relics that belonged to us, like the black-and-white photos nailed to the family room wall.

I could see the want in their dusk-lit eyes, the quarry dangling like bait. And from the natural smile on Brenda's face, I could see she had no idea how I was feeling, what was happening inside me. She would never be a true friend.

"When can we see it?" They all said. But seeing the quarry meant seeing my mother.

THERE WAS A TIME WHEN I was proud of the way she looked, with her Singer-sewn clothes in step with current fashions — polyester pants and matching tunics, brocade dresses. I loved to watch her dress for parties she and Dad used to have at the Upside-Down House. Dressed in her latest Vogue creation, she'd brush her short red hair and skillfully put on her make-up — Helena Rubinstein, Mary Quant. A halo-spray of her signature scent, Chanel No. 5. I wanted that cloud to give me her stylish beauty. The closest I got was a pink imprint on the cheek.

I remembered them dancing at the Upside-Down House. The living room, neat and tidy, ready for their parade of incoming guests. I'd already placed all the ashtrays out on the side tables, along with the bowls of mixed nuts and potato chips, onion dip and coasters. I was allowed to help. I was old enough to not drop things.

Elvis was on the record player. Mom's favourite song: "Blue Suede Shoes."

Tucked between the back of the sofa and the rungs of the banister, I was safe from their eyes and they were safe from mine. They could be themselves—alone—without me. I saw what they were together as the music played, a match of body and air as they moved in harmonic circles, their arms and legs knowing what to do. One needed the other to *be* the other. Even as a little girl I could see that.

Mom's upright grand came to life under her long-fingered hands. Everyone sang along. The joy in the mix of male and female voices seeped through the bedroom ceiling, becoming my lullaby. But this memory was fading into the silence of the lidded piano that now sat in the living room of our cedar-walled bungalow, shut like Mom's wooden-cased metronome.

The wig, the hunch, the stench from bedsores, the puffy skin and goggle sunglasses, the walker, the wheelchair, the needles and pills—these, the current fixtures of my house-bound mother.

I thought back to when she could drive, when the Malibu was hers. I was standing behind the glass doors of Ridgeway High after school hours, waiting for my lift home. I kept an eye out for Dad's blue Caddy, his comfort car, his highway office. He drove it up and down the QEW, visiting clients, selling envelopes to big companies. He needed a vehicle big enough to handle his back pain. Born with one leg longer than the other, he was told it was easy to fix with orthopaedic shoes. But he was never fitted with orthopaedic shoes or he refused to wear them, so his spine grew in crooked. He needed a vehicle big enough for his bones to breathe.

"It's for show," Nana had said, sucking her gold tooth. Crossing her arms, she'd stand deliberately by the living room window whenever he pulled the Caddy into the carport, between the Malibu and her gold Oldsmobile.

As I waited for Dad's Caddy, I was hoping I'd done well on my make-up test for physics. I'd missed the bus the day of the big test. Dad was on the road, visiting clients. Mom was too tired to drive me. Nana wasn't living with us then. I sat in Dad's home office, the room off the kitchen. His office was always packed with papers. Files and boxes of envelopes, the product he sold so well, covered Mom's cedar chest. Dad called it her hope chest. I doodled on his office calendar. Snails and happy faces beside his manic tornadoes. I wondered if he'd seen them. I'd forgotten to ask. *Today, I'll ask him. I must remember that.*

There were others waiting for lifts. Mouthy girls, pretty girls and jocks were clustered outside. I felt safe waiting inside on my own. And then it happened. I saw a green car with the top down, a red wig and those ugly goggle glasses. She pulled the Malibu into the arc of the driveway. All heads turned.

She was peering from group to group. When she saw I wasn't outside, she looked through the glass doors. I saw her puffy cheeks – round and squirrelly, chemo-helium balloons. She pushed the car horn. She was idling in the middle of the arc, so the next car, a Trans Am, couldn't pass. That car beeped. She waved then, a jerky motion. I knew she was rattled. She drove forward, then in reverse, almost hitting the Trans Am. That's when I rushed out. I snapped open the passenger door and hopped in, looked down at my physics textbook. But I wasn't looking at my book. I wasn't seeing a thing.

DURING ONE OF my afternoon shifts, Chuck came in and said to close the pool for the rest of the day. Men were arriving to test the water for chemicals.

I blew my whistle. "Everyone out now! Pool closes early today."

No one was happy about that.

"It's sooo hot," said Brenda. She'd come with me to suntan by the pool. It was her day off from selling donuts. She wanted to show off her new white bikini. She didn't care that her stomach showed. I could never do that.

After grabbing our stuff, we headed to the back field to find the boys. As we approached their huddle around the picnic table, the scent of marijuana grew stronger.

"Hey!" said Brenda. "We've been looking for you guys. Pool's closed. Let's go swimming in Caitlin's quarry."

I stopped walking.

They all turned to look at me. Their eyes bright and eager.

SEAN BORROWED his father's van and Brenda and the boys piled in. Darren rode with me. He was watching me drive, a toothy grin on his face. A half-hour earlier, when he checked my eyes, he said he couldn't see any red squiggles. Just the same, I'd slipped on sunglasses, the only pair I could find. It was the extra pair Mom had left in the glove compartment — those ugly goggle glasses.

"You're cute, little bug-eye," said Darren. "You're a little bug."

I couldn't believe I was wearing them. The joint had made that happen. He tugged the edge of his yellow bandana, which he'd knotted around my head. I kept my hands in the ten/two position. With all that smoke buzzing through me, my grip helped anchor the buzz.

When he'd first handed me the joint, the smoke hadn't slipped down like I'd thought it would.

"You inhale?" he asked. We were in the woods where the keg used to be, but with no nighttime to hide us. "Try again."

This time I inhaled too much and coughed. He rubbed circles on my back.

"Here, drink this."

I drank the rest of his Pepsi, something I never drink — too much sugar. But I needed to stop coughing, and with new sensations floating through me, I didn't care about the extra calories. "I'm ready now," I said after my last cough.

When he passed me the joint again, I put my lips to it and took a longer drag. I passed it back.

He inhaled the last bit. "Come on," he said, his voice clogged with smoke. "Let's see your quarry."

When I turned down Dominion Road, Sean flicked the van's high beams and my rear-view mirror caught his bursts of light. I had this urge to keep staring at the flashes, as if deciphering a code. I made myself stare ahead at the oncoming road. *Pay attention, Caitlin.* With the Malibu's top down, the sun oiled our skin and the wind slapped us. My throat ached for more Pepsi, and my stomach grumbled for food.

"Faster!" yelled Darren. He raised his arms as if we were riding the Comet, the roller coaster at the nearby amusement park, Crystal Beach. "Wahoo!" he said. He turned the radio on full blast. "Eye of the Tiger." We were off Dominion now, racing toward the railway tracks at the top of the little hill. My heart was beating fast through my *Lifeguard* T-shirt. I stepped on the gas.

The stern clarity of my father's voice – *always remember to slow down here* – was stifled by the pushing wind. I thought, *this is what it feels like meeting fate, willing fate* –

If a train had been coming, I wouldn't have stopped.

Moments later, while I barfed behind the bloomless lilac bushes by our driveway's bend, Darren ordered the others to wait in the van. "If she wasn't driving, she wouldn't be sick. Bad combination."

After the last dry heave, I wiped my mouth with some lilac leaves, took a deep breath and got back behind the wheel. My stomach was empty. That part felt good. Maybe I'd lost a pound or two, maybe more. But the inevitable was going to happen. I couldn't stop it.

Everyone oohed and aahed at the beauty of the quarry. They wanted to go for a swim. When we walked around the side of the house, we found Dad, Mom and Nana sitting outside. Mom in her wheelchair. Nana and Dad in the matching lawn chairs, a pair of hedge clippers by Dad's feet.

"What's wrong, Caitlin?" asked Mom. "You look green."

"I think I need to lie down."

"Who've we got here?" said Dad, standing up, looking at the group I'd brought home.

Darren introduced everyone, including Brenda.

"You already know Brenda," I said, cradling my stomach.

"I know I know Brenda. So, you're Darren?" Dad said, eyeing him.

The nausea had drained my bottled-up tension. I felt sick but I felt relaxed, too. Half the group avoided looking at Mom. The other half kept sneaking glances. Nana's knitting needles clicked. I knew Nana was watching me, even though

I was facing the quarry to catch the breeze, a wind-cloth on my face. "I think I need to lie down."

Darren took my arm and led me to Dad's empty lawn chair. "You need some water?" he asked.

"Honey," Mom said. "Let me feel your forehead."

"Take that thing off," said Dad. "Your mother can't feel your forehead with that thing on. Where'd you get it, anyway?"

I pushed the yellow bandana up off my forehead and leaned toward Mom's wheelchair. Felt her cool, thin hand on my skin.

"She's a bit warm, Don."

"Too much sun," said Nana.

"Where's that visor I got you?" said Dad. "Are those your mother's sunglasses?"

"They want to swim," I said. "Can they?"

"When you need to lie down? Dave, go get Caitlin some water, will ya? Go on. Go in the house. Glasses are in the cupboard, beside the sink."

"Darren," said Darren.

"What about Darren?" asked Dad.

"Don, his name is Darren," said Mom. "Remember?"

"I said Darren, didn't I?" He looked at my friends, the awkward cluster. "Geez, you're all so quiet. Are you always so quiet? They can come back and swim another time," he said, looking at me. He turned to the door. "Where's that glass of water?"

So they left. Bulldog, Sean, JP, Brenda. But not Darren. Dad made Darren stay.

"I'll give you a lift back to Hideaway. You can help me wash the Caddy."

I lay in my bedroom in the curtained dark, the single bed like a rocking boat. I felt for my hip bones. Too much flesh. Between the oncoming waves of nausea came the sound of spraying water outside the hallway window, of hose-water hitting metal, and above that my father's voice. "You missed another spot. That a boy. You gotta rub hard to get the bugs out."

When I woke up, the room was pitch black, my mouth dry and pasty. I went to the bathroom, brushed away the weedy taste, climbed back to bed. When I woke again, it was morning.

"What's wrong with that boy?" Dad said from his office. I was waiting for my Pop-Tart to pop out of the toaster. "Doesn't he know how to wash a car? Left soap film everywhere. Had to rinse it all over again."

"What are you talking about?" I said, rubbing my head. Yesterday's dull throb was coming back.

"Shh," he said. "I'm on the phone." And he closed his office door.

"Your dad's a bully," Darren said during my morning break. "Jesus. Watched me like a hawk. *You missed a spot.* Over and over. Gave me nothing to drink. Had to drink from the goddamn hose."

"I'm sorry," I said.

"What ya have to go and get sick for?"

"I couldn't help it."

"Didn't I show you how to inhale? Next time watch. Watch closely."

The hurt in my head accelerated. I pulled down my visor and sipped my Diet Coke to stifle the nausea that kept shifting through me. Just the thought of that weedy smell.

"There won't be a next time."

"What do you mean? You barely tried it. Don't worry," he said, squeezing my shoulders. "You'll try again."

"WE NEED TO TALK," said Dad. It was morning and I was getting ready to leave for my Saturday shift at Hideaway. "Let's sit on the dock."

"I don't have time, Dad."

"You have time." He stirred a packet of Equal into his favourite coffee mug. It was the ceramic one Mom had given him, before the walker and the wheelchair, when she could play the game she excelled at. He'd laughed when he read the words on the mug: Old tennis players never die they just lose their balls. "Grab your Pop-Tart and come on."

The water was still as dew. Everything doubled into the quarry. Water bugs skated across the tight surface. Fluffs of cottonwood floated.

"He's an interesting fellow, your Dave."

"Darren, Dad."

"Yeah, Darren. A little rough around the edges though, isn't he? Street smart?"

"He's from Buffalo."

"Whereabouts?"

"Near the river, just over the Peace Bridge."

"Not too far from Chef's then, eh?" He smacked his lips as if he'd just swallowed the cheese-lidded pasta the Italian restaurant was famous for. "Not the best part of town. So he's only here for the summer?"

"His parents have a campsite, a trailer. It's cool."

"No summer job."

"He does. He does odd jobs around the campground.

He painted the pool sign."

He eyed the arrow hanging from my neck. "He give you that?"

I smiled and fingered the silver point.

"If he's from Buffalo, you know it won't last."

"Dad!"

"I'm just saying ... we don't want you to get hurt."

"We?"

"Me and your mother."

"Mom likes Darren."

Dad sipped his coffee.

"She told me," I said, when he didn't answer. "And she thinks you were too hard on him."

"I think you're a bit confused here. She wants you to be happy. He won't make you happy."

"He does make me happy."

"By smoking dope?"

"What are you talking about?"

"I saw his eyes."

"You don't know anything," I said, tossing the last of my Pop-Tart in the water. A rise of sunfish frenzied for it, little mouths of 'O'. "I'm going now," I said, standing up.

He scanned my body. "Have you lost weight?"

"No," I said, patting my stomach. The bathroom scale had proved it this morning. "I wish."

"Take the Caddy. I want the convertible. It's gonna be a nice day."

He knew I hated driving his Caddy, that big lug of metal that signalled: *look at me.*

"I'd rather ride my bike."

He looked at his watch. "You'll be late then," he said.

DESPITE DARREN'S ON-AGAIN, off-again dope-smoking habit and my refusal to try it again, we stayed together that summer. He had strategies for our soon-to-be long-distance relationship – a phone card. Where he'd gotten the phone card, he wouldn't say. Would phone calls be enough?

"See?" said Darren. "That's my point. Drive to Buffalo. Come and see me. You have a car."

I did have a car, yes. Well, Mom's car. But I wasn't allowed to drive it across the border, and he knew that.

"So? Don't tell your dad."

"But what if he finds out?"

"What's the worst he could do? Ground you?"

"Can't you come see *me*?"

"And how would I get there and where would we hang out? At the quarry with your dad all over me?"

"We could drive somewhere."

"You know it makes sense to come to Buffalo. My parents don't hassle. We don't have to hide." He kissed my neck to make me shiver. "You don't have to do everything he says, you know."

AFTER LABOUR DAY crashed into our lives, I lived for his phone calls. He called from different phone booths at different times; he didn't want to get caught. After his phone card ran out, he tapped into someone's private line. I didn't care if it was illegal. I needed to hear his voice. I sat near a phone before his calls, waiting. This was becoming awkward, with Mom resting in her hospital bed by the bedroom phone, or Nana cooking in the kitchen by the kitchen phone, or Dad working in his office by the office phone. Fortunately, Dad didn't stay very long in his office when he arrived home from work. Once he changed out of his suit and tie and into his casual clothes, he had his daily chat with Mom by her bedside, and then off he went to see Louie, his childhood buddy from Baie-D'Urfé. They watched games together – baseball or hockey, in bars where they drank beers. Games he used to watch at home before Nana came to live with us.

While waiting for the telephone to ring, I imagined Darren stepping into a phone booth, a smile on his face, and dialling my number. I imagined him in that phone booth thinking of me – missing me, wanting to hold me, kiss me, touch me. I knew he wanted more. I'd promised I would by Labour Day. Something kept holding me back.

"Don't you love me?" he'd said our last night together. He'd be leaving for Buffalo the next day.

"Of course I do." I thought I could that night. I wanted to. But when he lowered his hand, I jumped.

"Jesus, Caitlin. It's only sex."

I could barely say the word "sex" without blushing. The one-syllable word was a grenade like "dick" or "cunt." As a little girl I knew not to say these words, even before I knew their meanings. Their taboo brought a pucker to the mouth.

But some words were too secret to be taboo.

During our first year at the quarry, I was sitting with Mom in the family room, thinking of the word the cool girls whispered as they made their way to the back of the school bus. I'd never heard the word before. Would Mom know it? She was watching her favourite show, *National Geographic*, while sewing. Blobs of jellyfish bloomed across the television screen. The dark ocean highlighted their fleshy colours, illuminating them from within, as if tiny sea-suns had pummelled through them. Liquid grace. Hard to imagine those harsh stings. She was making me a witch costume from the same Butterick pattern that had made me a princess the year before.

"Mom, what's an orgasm?"

"Ouch," she said, and sucked her finger, her blue eyes wide, as if she'd suddenly been threatened by a bigger animal.

"What?" I leaned on the arm of the chesterfield and pinched the biggest charm on my bracelet, the silver horse. I made it ride my skin.

"It's something that happens... to some women... sometimes."

"Happens? To you?"

She made a thin line with her lips. She didn't want to tell me.

They were pulsing now, the jellyfish, in a gluey mass.

She went back to sewing my witch's cape for Halloween.

I was probably too old for trick-or-treating, but I wanted free candy. Mom had told Dad she'd take me. She could still drive then, even though she'd had the "woman's operation."

There were few houses around the forested quarry, so Mom drove the Malibu down to Crescent Park, a subdivision where identical houses stood on square plots. Smaller than the ones in Grimsby, but plots nonetheless. I kept thinking I'd see a familiar face when the front door opened. I didn't know our Grimsby neighbours by name, but I knew their faces. I missed the Upside-Down House terribly that first year.

I was one of the tallest trick-or-treaters roaming the dark streets, so maybe it was a good thing they didn't know me. You can hide a lot wearing a witch costume, like the stomach I hated, but you can't hide height.

That night Mom came to my bedroom.

"Here," she said, and she passed me a stapled blue pamphlet. "I'd like you to read this."

I was on top of my bed eyeing my loot, strategizing — what to save, what to eat first — and how to manage the calories. "What's this?" I said with no interest. When I picked up the pamphlet, I saw my age in black bold letters: *Dr. Harry Talks to a Twelve-Year-Old About Sex.*

After she left the room, I opened it.

I was glad I didn't have a penis, a hose that got hard and spat stuff out. It looked lost hanging there. Like it wanted to go somewhere but was tied to its hairy nest. My parts were coddled inside, safe. But the pamphlet revealed a hole I didn't know I had. I went to the bathroom and locked the door, shimmied out of my flowered underwear.

Nothing happened when I touched inside it. I didn't feel my insides go 'O' the way they did when I rubbed higher, between the pink flaps, a slow and steady rub that made me rise in waves, up and out, a rub that expanded, the complete opposite of the rub of a Pink Pearl eraser, a rub which made things disappear, forever.

The pamphlet didn't have the word "orgasm" but the dictionary did: *to swell with moisture, lust; the climax of sexual excitement, as in intercourse, usually accompanied in the male by ejaculation.* I liked my orgasm. It was clean, quiet.

I STARED AT THE PHONE in the master bedroom, waiting for Darren to make it ring. Mom would be starting another round of radiation soon. *She's a fighter, your mother,* Dad always said. We knew she'd be okay. She always came through. *Cancer will be beaten* read the button from the Cancer Society. It sat on the chipped saucer with Dad's small change. *She never wears it.* I was thinking this as I sat on the king-sized bed, trying not to smell the growing presence that lingered in her bedsheets. I kept waiting and waiting for the phone to ring.

The second week after Labour Day, I heard a quiet knock at our side door. When I went to answer it, there was Darren, his blond curls meshed by screen, his sidekick Sean standing behind him, shuffling his feet. I was expecting Darren to call that night, not for him to show up in person.

"What are you guys doing here?" I tossed my wet tea towel on the kitchen counter. No time to fix my hair or smear Bonne Bell Lip Smacker over my lips. When I opened the screen door, they didn't move. "Come in before the bugs do. You too, Sean."

"He'll wait outside," Darren said, still standing there. He looked over at the carport, "Your dad's out, I see. This won't take long." He stepped past the vestibule threshold without closing the door. The light from the kitchen became a moon for moths, a moon of false light. They winged past us, carrying crisp air.

"I'm seeing someone."

"You're what?"

"It's too hard. You, here. Me, there." He pointed to the quarry.

"Buffalo's the other way."

"You know what I mean."

"Oh, so she's from Buffalo, then? I bet she smokes dope." I looked at the whites of his eyes, but the light wasn't strong enough to check for redness. "You said we'd make this work. How did you get here?"

Sean gave a little wave, a little flag of surrender.

"You're a great girl," said Darren. "It's been great knowing you." When he leaned toward me, a moth fluttered over his head.

I thought he was going to kiss me on the mouth and say, "Joking!" But he pushed back the yellow bandana to kiss the centre of my forehead, where the third eye lives. An eye that must be blind, as I hadn't seen any of this coming.

"Keep it," he said, acknowledging the bandana. He eyed my neck, the silver arrow. "I need that back. Okay?"

I unfastened the clasp—I was surprised my fingers could do that—and passed him the necklace. He stuffed it into the inside pocket of his jean jacket. We didn't say goodbye. He left the door open, and the moths fluttered in.

Five minutes later, when the side door opened again, in came Dad, swinging his car keys. I was drying the dishes that were already dry, making them damp with my wet tea towel.

"Jesus," he said. "Almost got hit around the goddamn corner. Who the hell was that?"

DAD WAS DRIVING ME to school a lot this spring. With a spare first period, I had a later start this term, my last one before graduation. The trees were about to burst leaves of electric green. Nature's neon. Soon dandelions would flower, followed by ghostly seeds, mini-parachutes. I still had the yellow bandana. I kept it coiled in the top drawer of my bureau between my socks and underwear, proof I did have a boyfriend, it did happen, it wasn't a dream. Dad popped another Rolaids in his mouth and fiddled with the shoulder strap of his unbuckled seat belt. "You should fasten it, Dad. It's the law now."

"You know it hurts my back." He looked at my belt and nodded his approval. I never left mine unfastened like he did, the shoulder strap pulled loosely over his chest, his foil for passing cop cars. He stopped his sucking to chew.

"So? What do you think of this beauty?"

I breathed in the new-car smell. "I saw it yesterday, Dad. It's nice." I didn't dare mention what I'd heard Nana say when he arrived home in his new Caddy, a blue Eldorado to replace the two-year-old blue Seville. *Another one? Who's he trying to impress? And why the new clothes?* She didn't appreciate Dad's philosophy: *looking good is the key to life.* And yet Nana knew how to look good. She always looked good. She made herself shine like the silver cutlery she polished, the knick-knacks she constantly dusted. She didn't like his style but Mom did. She loved to see Dad all dressed up, looking dapper, freshly shaven, smelling good.

Dad squeezed the leather steering wheel with both hands. "Nice? That's all you can say? But you weren't riding in it yesterday. Smoother ride, eh? Bigger. More room. Watch this." He pushed a button and the outside mirror shifted with a slow mechanical swivel. "And feel," he said, rubbing the plush seat. "That smell." He breathed in deeply. "Don't you love that smell?"

"It's a good smell," I said, rubbing the plush. "It's a nice car, Dad."

He smiled.

Dad's fashionable clothes hung next to Mom's new clothes, ugly baggy dresses that she was forced to wear, that didn't constrain her pain-riddled body. These hung next to Mom's never-worn-anymore clothes, Vogue, Simplicity and Butterick fashions that gave me good mother memories

—when she could whack a tennis ball across the court and dress up pretty for a night on the town or for those dinner parties they used to have in Grimsby. Closet proof she wasn't always like this—pumped with pills, groggy and bent, pale and tired, bedridden. Clothes on hangers, waiting for the wearer to be well again.

Nana never let Dad forget what she'd given up to help with Mom's home care. Away from her busy life in Owen Sound, she no longer had curling in winter, golfing in summer, her Imperial Order Daughter of the Empire meetings, and deliveries for Meals on Wheels, or her special seat in St. Andrew's Presbyterian Church, third pew to the right (no one would dare sit there during her absence). Nana Florence came into my life the years the Brants were no longer part of it—my cousins, my aunt and uncle. As if life required some kind of emptiness and familial refilling.

I had no early memories of Nana. There'd been a falling-out. "You were a baby then," Mom had said before Nana's arrival at the quarry. "And sure, Nana's come 'round, hasn't she? You used to see her in Owen Sound when you were a little girl, remember?"

Why did we stop going? So many gaps with Nana. There and not there.

Just like my Lambie.

She never did say she was sorry for throwing Lambie out. I'd left her behind during our last visit to Owen Sound. With the Gravol pill inside me—Mom had made sure I'd taken one after breakfast for the long drive home—and Nana's horrible cream of wheat sat like a rock in my gut, I fell asleep in the back seat of the Buick. When I opened my eyes, we were nearing our house in Grimsby. The Niagara Escarpment rose like the gentle stomach of a sleeping giant. I squeezed my hand as if squeezing the neck of Lambie—

Mom!

"It's unhygienic, Mary Ellen," I'd heard Nana say the morning of our departure. "Besides, she's a little old now, isn't she?"

I hated this memory.

They'd go for weeks without talking to each other in that red brick house Mom grew up in. Nana mad at Mary Ellen (she never called her daughter Rusty) and Mom mad at Nana. Those cruel bouts of silence, from Mom's early childhood into young adulthood, were initiated by Nana. Mom had to wait for her mother to come around. All pleas and apologies were ignored, and with a husband away for months on end, captaining a freighter through the Great Lakes, Nana ruled what happened at that house. Such bouts of pointed silence never happened to Mom's younger brother, Tom. Thomas Maharg. Nana's favourite. He lived in the Far East now. We never saw him.

It took Mom's cancer to make Nana soften. Why else would she be here? When she first arrived at the quarry, Nana brought things from the red brick house, some Maharg family treasures: Blue Willow dishes and a pair of antique dolls.

Mom smiled when she received them. Her eyes welled to the same shade of blue. "Lovely," she said, holding a plate, seeking her reflection.

I knew the story behind the Blue Willow. One of the plates used to sit on the shelf above the sink in the turquoise kitchen at the Upside-Down House. It was the only story I could remember Mom telling me as she sat by my bedside and soothed me to sleep.

Many, many years ago, long before you were born, there lived a widowed queen. This widowed queen lived in a big brick house with her beautiful daughter, Blue. When it was time for Blue to leave the house, the queen made arrangements for Blue to marry a very rich man, a clever man, a captain of a ship. When the Captain met Blue, he was very happy. When Blue met the Captain, she was not. He was old, ugly and bossy. He smelled bad, too.

One day, Blue went out for a walk in the nearby park to sit near the water. She liked to be near water. It helped soothe the deep pit of sadness that lived inside her. While she sat there, lost in her thoughts, a young man walked by. A tall, talkative, handsome man. He sat down and they started talking, and they fell in love. "I want to marry you," he said. She told him she couldn't. She ran away crying.

The wedding day came, and the Captain and Blue were married. Blue was very sad. She cried and cried, and the tears she cried made a river, and this river made its way back to the Handsome Man. "Yes," he said when he saw the river. He built a boat and set it on the river, and the river led him back to Blue. "You're here," he said, and she said that too. They hugged each other and wouldn't let go. Luckily, the Captain was travelling the Great Lakes, so he didn't see Blue hugging the Handsome Man; he didn't see his wife step into the Handsome Man's boat and sail away with him to a secret island. But when the Captain came home and discovered his wife wasn't there, he was furious. He vowed he would find her and take back what was his.

Blue and the Handsome Man were happy living together on their secret island. They loved to watch the water glitter with sunlight. They thought they were safe. The Captain would never find them. They felt this way for a long time.

One day, they went for a walk, and when they happened to turn around – they both had a bad feeling – they saw the Captain running toward them. He was carrying a big, sharp knife. He was closer now; he almost had them, he was only an arm's length away. The couple ran and ran, and they ran so fast that their running lifted them off the ground and into the air, and their arms grew wings. They'd turned into birds.

She handed me the Blue Willow dish from the turquoise kitchen and pointed to the two birds in flight at the top of the plate. "Doves," she said. "Mourning doves."

I was thinking of Blue and the Handsome Man as Dad fiddled with the rear-view mirror. Up ahead on the telephone wire sat a pair of mourning doves.

Dad straightened his paisley tie and said, "So you're going to McMaster, the one in Hamilton, next year. Toronto's too far away."

"You mean U of T's too big. What about Guelph? It's smaller."

"I mean you need to be near your mother. And you'll need money for tuition. Supposed to be a rainy summer," he said, looking up. He didn't see the birds. We'd already passed them. "You won't get enough hours at that pool."

I could see him looking at me, waiting for my reaction. I kept my eyes on the telephone wires. I wanted to see more birds.

"I'll set you up with Louie selling bus tours in Niagara Falls, a job on commission. You won't have to see that Dave guy again." He squeezed my knee.

"Darren," I said, pulling my knee away from him. The rest of the wires sat empty.

QT

I FELT LIKE A STRANGER on Clifton Hill, standing behind a wooden booth positioned near the driveway entrance to Niagara Clifton Motor Inn. Glass-encased photos highlighted the places tourists would visit on Louie's bus tour: Spanish Aero Car, Floral Clock, Niagara Gorge, Whirlpool Rapids and, of course, the ultimate wonder, Niagara Falls. Between the American and the Canadian Falls, our Horseshoe was the bigger of the two. Nighttime photos showcased the light pageantry, rainbow illuminations of the tumbling water.

Horseshoe Falls was ours and would always be ours. Rich Americans couldn't take it away from us the way they'd taken prime beachfront property along our Lake Erie shoreline with their summer cottages as big as houses, leaving locals with measly strips of public beach. Once the winter weather turned warm, our small town became their summer play-ground, our beach their backyard.

With all the noises and flashing lights, I felt like I was standing inside a giant arcade, far from the natural beauty at the end of this crowded, hilly street. The Hill was a world of its own, a hub of nationalities with tourists from around the world – all shapes, sizes and accents – exploring tacky museums: The House of Frankenstein, Ripley's Believe It or Not!, Guinness Book of World Records, Louis Tussaud's Wax Museum. Plus souvenir shops and fast-food joints. I felt dizzy and misplaced.

I didn't know what to do behind the booth, facing a street full of strangers. I was afraid to talk to potential ticket buyers. When they looked at me, I looked away. The job was commission-only. It was Dad's fault I wasn't working at Hideaway Park Campground.

At least I wouldn't have to face Darren again. A kiss on the forehead. I should've punched him in the face.

Louie stood behind me, under the veranda of the Niagara Clifton Motor Inn, talking to Dad. They both had salt-and-pepper hair, but Louie's comb-over couldn't hide his pink bald spot. From the bronze sheen of his face, I guessed he used the same sunless tanning lotion that Dad did: QT. Quick Tan.

"You should use it, Caitlin," said Dad whenever he noticed how pale I was and whenever I smeared it over his back, something Mom used to do but couldn't any longer. Once I forgot to wash my hands.

"Look," I said, holding up my orange palms as if a gun were pointed at my back. "That's what your stuff does to me."

"Kiddo," said Louie, suddenly standing beside me. I jumped. Surrounded by so much activity, I hadn't heard him approaching. "You're a jittery one, aren't you? There's someone I want you to meet." He nudged the short man beside him. "Ted, say hello to the girl."

When Ted removed his flashy Ray-Bans, his squinting squeezed his crow's feet. He barely came up to Louie's broad shoulders, but his white hair was thick, every strand perfectly in place. Like Dad's hair after he sprayed The Dry Look over it. A prerequisite for selling, maybe? Dad always kept an extra can inside his glove compartment for emergency touch-ups.

"You're at my booth," Ted said.

"But Louie told me—"

"Quit teasing her." Louie chuckled. "You weren't here, so she used it. Ted's going to show you what to do. I'm going to grab a bite with your Daddy-O."

Dad stood under the veranda talking on Louie's outdoor phone. As young men they used to sell envelopes together at Dominion Envelope until Louie went solo and began his own business—Niagara Falls Scenic Bus Tours. "He likes the tacky trade," Dad had said during our drive down the QEW, after his pep talk that didn't pep me up. He didn't know Aunt Doris had already told me about Louie. Dad's childhood friend had caused his near-drowning. Somehow they'd managed to keep their friendship going since that time. I tried not to think about Cindy.

I waved at Dad. He didn't wave back. He kept talking on the phone. *Didn't he see me?* Who was he talking to? Mom? No, Mom would be having her pre-lunch nap. Nana kept her to a tight routine.

Louie pointed to the giant plastic vanilla ice-cream cone across the street. "You can eat after us. Get a hot dog or something." He looked me up and down. "Get some meat on your bones."

"WELL," SAID TED, "with you being easy on the eyes and all —that should help. Let's see your smile."

I didn't feel like smiling. I gave a half-smile.

"Yeah, okay. Show your teeth. You gotta look sincere." He tapped the booth. "These here photos bring tourists in, but if you're standing too close, they won't approach. You gotta stand back, just a little."

I stepped back.

"Not now, when you're working the booth. When they do wander in, you step in slow, see?" He stepped forward with exaggerated steps like a man on the moon. "Beautiful Floral Clock, isn't it?"

I couldn't see the photo from where I was standing. I stepped closer.

"What are you doing?"

"I'm looking at the Floral Clock." I thought of Mom standing beside the Floral Clock during our first family trip to the falls, smiling for Dad's camera. She'd wanted me in the photo too, but Dad had said, "Just you, Russ."

Ted fanned the emptiness around him. "I'm talking to Flo Tourist. She's here with her hubby, Fred." He fanned more air. "Get it? When that happens, you don't need a hook. You let these photos do the work." He thumped the glass with his fist. Rings circled most of his fingers, gold like the chains that hung around his hairy neckline. He was wearing more jewelery than Dad and me combined.

A woman heading down The Hill, young boys on either side of her, stopped and pointed upwards to the fibreglass yellow-caped tightrope walker balanced on a wire. "Funambulist," said Ted, looking at the high-wire dummy. "Bet you didn't know that, eh?"

"No, I didn't know that."

A man in a neon-pink T-shirt caught Ted's eye. He smiled at Ted. Ted smiled back. Was Ted blushing? Hard to tell with that tan. Ted stuck his hand inside the booth and pulled out a brochure. "Phew, it's hot," he said, fanning his chin with the flimsy paper. "You hot?"

I nodded but he was already looking the other way. He opened the brochure. "Been a while since I read this. Forgot about that." He flipped it over. "All in here now," he said, and tapped his creased forehead. He handed me the brochure. "Here's tonight's homework. Memorize it." He jiggled his pocket and pulled out some coins. "I was gonna treat you, but there's just enough for one can," he said, eyeing the nearby Coca-Cola machine. Little beads of sweat hugged his upper lip. "Jesus, it's hot today. You hot?"

While Ted wandered up to the Coca-Cola machine, I thought back to my first visit to Niagara Falls. I must've been six or seven. The gorge water was moving in sluggish half-circles, snake-like. "The current," Mom had called it. "Deadly." We must've walked up the Niagara Parkway after that, for what came next was mist on my arms and face. It mixed with the sweat the sun had coaxed out of me. We weaved through the crowd of all skin colours and unfamiliar accents, toward the stone-fenced edge. "Look," Dad said, holding me up. The fast-running water folded over the edge of the falls, which curved like our chesterfield, in a steady flow, smooth like a conveyer belt, endless. When Dad's arms tired, Mom took over. Cloaked in her cloud of Chanel No. 5 and old cigarette smoke, I felt the mist tickling my face.

I MEMORIZED THE BROCHURE that night, and the facts were fresh in my head when I woke up. I'd score perfect on a quiz. Ted wouldn't. He wouldn't remember that the nightly illuminations began in 1925 or that the Floral Clock was made up of sixteen thousand carpet bedding plants.

I thought of that photo of Mom by the Floral Clock. *Did she remember that day? Would asking her only remind her of all the things her body couldn't do anymore?* Mom loved flowers. Especially impatiens and begonias, the annuals that bordered our brown bungalow, a gift each spring from one of Dad's best accounts, Statler Seeds. She never asked for my help when the flowers arrived in late May. She liked to plant them on her own.

This year, like last year, Nana had done the planting. She used a ruler for spacing, something Mom never did. Thankfully, the blooms spread like the renegade dandelions that needled through the gravel driveway. They filled up Nana's regimented spaces. But the hot sun cracked the dirt, demanding daily watering. My job. One I hated—lugging the hose from one end of the L-shaped bungalow to the other, filling up the plastic bucket off the dock for the hard-to-reach blooms. Boring and time-consuming. I was tired after my first day of work. What I wanted to do was swim.

"You'll swim when you're done," Dad said.

But every day? Couldn't the flowers wait?

"Dry as pitch," Mom said, eyeing the cracked earth. There was a little smack from her pursing lips, as if she could feel the roots' thirst.

TURNS OUT Ted didn't want me at his lucky booth. "Fresh meat," he called tourists who'd just checked in. Louie stationed me behind another booth, farther from the action.

"It's the only one we got right now," Louie said and shrugged his shoulders.

After two hours of watching strangers walk by, up and down Clifton Hill, I left my booth for my mid-morning break. I walked past Ted's booth and pumped coins into the Coca-Cola machine. Sipping my Diet Coke, I stepped away from the machine's humming to listen to his spiel. He was talking to a young Asian couple about things that weren't in the brochure. How Superman saved Lois Lane from the Whirlpool Rapids' treachery. How the first person to tightrope walk across the Niagara Gorge was a Frenchman who called himself The Great Blondin (the fibreglass yellow-caped daredevil?). "That's right, folks, Blondin even pushed a wheelbarrow to the centre of the rope, where he stopped, cooked an omelette on a small stove and ate it. Carried his manager on his back. Once he even crossed blindfolded!" His spiel then turned to the story of the old scow. Loaded with rock, the scow was being towed by a hydro tug to the upper river when the line broke. "Because the bottom grounded in time, the men were saved from the brink."

I'd seen the barge. It had shrubs growing out of it.

Memorize the points in the brochure? A boring list of facts? Ted's *helpful* advice? He was telling stories. He was making them see.

As my workday neared its end, I hadn't sold one ticket. The closest I came was an older couple who promised they'd be back. They wanted the night-illumination tour. They loved the photos showing the rainbow effect over cascading water.

Niagara Falls lit like magic. My first sale was going to happen, I was sure of it. But it was almost time to go, and they hadn't come back yet.

On my way to Mom's Malibu, I saw the couple standing under the verandah. They were waiting with others for the evening tour bus to arrive.

"Hello! You need a ticket," I said, my heart racing with excitement. *Wait until I share this with Dad.*

The woman waved a ticket and pointed to Ted, standing by his booth. "He gave us a special discount."

"Fucking Ted," I muttered under my breath.

Driving home that night, I stopped at the library and checked out all the books on Niagara Falls I could find. I couldn't cure my shyness, but I could learn the stories behind the facts, spill them out like a waterfall. With all the new trivia stuffed inside me, I came up with an idea. I'd make a questionnaire. A *did-you-know* sheet. Use it as a hook.

Dad loved the idea. We were sitting on the dock watching the sunset after he'd watched me swim my evening lengths, back and forth between the dock and the floating raft. Mom was inside the house with Nana. Another evening she was too tired to come out. But she couldn't sit and do nothing, so she sat on the chesterfield making crafts—calico mice, fabric purses, stuffed Christmas trees—items she put toward Quarry Crafts, the charity she'd started for the United Church.

Once a week during the school year, a group of church ladies used our family room as a sewing room. Eleanor and others followed Mom's lead, watching the magic she worked with her hands, and when Reverend Barker dropped by, they all stopped for tea and homemade squares. "Come and join us, Caitlin," they said when I arrived home from school, except for Carol, who kept to herself. Dressed in long-sleeved blouses, was she hiding more bruises?

Mom was always focused on her latest handiwork. Except for the permanent curve of her spine, she resembled her old self, from a distance. That glow on her face. She thrived on the room's energy. She held court like a kind queen bee. Nana always eyed my plate to see how many treats I'd taken from the ladies' tins. *Don't spoil your dinner*, said her watchful look. I only took small bites of each square before throwing them out. I couldn't tell Nana that. She'd scold me for being wasteful. She never criticized the church ladies or gave them the "Nana eye." She smiled and chuckled with ease in their company. "Florence, you're a doll," they said.

Mom's silence wasn't calculating or withholding like Nana's. It never made you nervous. Being nervous meant you made mistakes—what Nana wanted. Mom's was an accepting silence. When we lived in Grimsby, while Mom sewed in the sewing room, I played with my dolls and stuffed animals on my bedroom floor. While Mom baked cookies in the turquoise kitchen, I sat at the kitchen table drawing birds and flowers. We shared our silence, immersed in our separate worlds. We didn't intrude on each other. And when the time for showing came—"Look, Mom! Look!"—she was there to see. She was present. We understood the showing part wasn't where the deepest pleasure lived. That was in the doing and making.

I fingered the questionnaire I'd attached to my clipboard. "I haven't tried it yet, Dad. I don't know if it'll work." I flipped through my notes. "Did you know the first person who went over the falls in a barrel was a woman? Annie Edson Taylor. A schoolteacher. And she was old! Over sixty."

"*Old?* Watch it, kiddo." He slapped his knee. "Jesus, this

takes me back. The planning, the execution, closing the deal. People think selling's easy, but it's not, eh? See that fish jump? That's what you want. Get their interest and you're halfway there. Establish some rapport and hook them in."

I watched the water rings dissolve. "But how do you deal with the rejection? It's awful when they walk away or say no to your face."

"It has nothing to do with you. Sometimes people don't want what you got." He shook his head. "Sometimes people are stupid."

"Ted plays with the prices, you know. He doesn't charge them all the same. That doesn't seem right."

Dad laughed. "You do what it takes to get bums on the bus. That's the name of the game. Besides, some people have more cash in their pockets. Look at their clothes, their jewelry. Suss them out."

I looked at Dad's hands. What would I see if I didn't know him? Tanned skin and dark hairs at the knuckles, tiger-eye ring, gold bracelet shiny like his polished Caddy, leather-strapped watch with Roman numerals.

"Did you tell your mother this?"

"You know I haven't. When would I have told her?" I hiked my towel up around my shoulders to stop the sudden chill. "You said I had to swim now—"

"Listen. Don't blame me for not spending time with your mother. You're always rushing off. Did you ask her how her day was? Sit and talk with her, for God's sake." He checked his watch. "Come on. Go get yourself changed. I gotta go."

"You're going out? What about dinner?"

"I'll grab a bite with Louie while we're watching the game."

Did you sit with Mom? Did you?

THE NEXT DAY I took hold of my clipboard and headed out in front of my booth. A middle-aged, plump couple dressed in matching T-shirts – *Virginia Is for Lovers* – stood there holding hands.

"Hello, there. Excuse me. Do you have a moment? I'm doing a little survey and would appreciate your help. Is this your first time visiting Niagara Falls?"

"Yes," said the woman, squeezing the man's generous waistline. They both wore wedding bands.

"Newlyweds?"

They smiled.

"Have I got a deal for you," I said with as much enthusiasm as I could generate. I headed back around the booth. *Please follow.* Once there, I dared to look up. They were staring at the glass-encased photos. A charge of excitement surged through me.

"Yes, you'll see all these beautiful sights and more on our fabulous tour. You won't have to worry about driving." I gestured to the bumper-to-bumper traffic behind them. "Or finding a place to park – what a nightmare. Parking is so expensive here. And…" I leaned forward and whispered, "Because you're on your honeymoon, I'll give you a special deal." I opened the brochure and pointed to the price. "Two for one. But you have to buy your tickets now."

I held my breath. *Should I give them more information? No, wait. Don't be pushy.*

"Sweetie, we should do this," the woman said. She unzipped her purse and took out her wallet. "My treat. You did all that driving. Here," she said and handed me the cash. "Looks like Monopoly money."

"Thank you," I said, taking the bills. "Thank you so much."

She stood waiting.

"Thank you," I repeated. *Why is she staring at me?*

"Don't we need tickets? Or do we just show up with our sweet smiling faces?"

"Yes. Oh, yes." I looked inside the booth and found a pack.

"Here you go." I felt giddy and light, as if I were floating. So this is how Dad felt after a sale.

TWO DAYS INTO my newfound success, Ted wandered down the hill. "What's that you got there?" He grabbed the clipboard I'd set on my booth and started reading my questionnaire. "You make this up?"

"I didn't make it up."

"Your dad then, eh?"

I wanted to grab the clipboard back, but I tried to be cool like the Diet Coke I was sipping. Was he jealous of my newfound technique?

"You sure this is legal? A bogus questionnaire? Might rattle the authorities, I mean, no organization behind it. Who's the questionnaire for?" He cupped his mouth and whispered, "Does Louie know about this?"

"No," I said, trying to hide my fluster. When I stepped back, my elbow hit the booth's corner and the Diet Coke went flying. "Shit!"

"Here." Ted handed me a hanky with his initials: TB.

I dabbed my white jeans. The stain was shaped like a Rorschach ink blot. A soda-pop Rorschach. *What do you see in me?* I saw failure that won't go away.

"I'd hide this for now," Ted said, and he tucked the clipboard inside my booth. "Good thing I found it before the big guy did." He glanced toward the veranda, where Louie stood talking on the phone. "He's gonna move you."

"Move me?"

When Louie saw Ted looking, he clasped the receiver. "Leave the girl alone," he shouted.

Ted saluted our boss, then winked at me. He looked at my thigh. "Still there, kiddo."

I dabbed the stain before handing him back his hanky.

"Keep it. Plenty more where that came from." He looked up The Hill. A couple with cameras looped around their necks had stopped at his booth.

"Hello there, folks!" said Ted, his short legs rushing toward them. "Which beautiful sight has caught your eye? Floral Clock? Did you know there are over sixteen thousand carpet flowers planted to make it bloom like that? What's that? No, clock's not anywhere near here but we have some comfy transport that will take you to the hidden gem."

I touched the stain. It was no longer wet – the humidity had absorbed it. But the hanky was chunky in the middle. "Gross," I said, dropping it.

"CAITLIN, HONEY?" Mom called from the master bedroom. I'd just arrived home from work and she must've heard me come in. When I entered the room, she was pushing her hips up, moving her shoulders, trying to get comfortable on the hospital bed.

I rearranged the pillows behind her head. "How's that?"

She tested for comfort. "Perfect." She smiled. "How was your day? Sell many?"

"Where's Nana?"

"Napping. She didn't sleep well last night."

Mom tipped the bendy straw, rimmed with pink, toward her mouth and sipped her water.

"Your nails look pretty, Mom." They matched her lipstick. I sat down on the king-sized bed and shifted to avoid seeing my reflection in the mirror. The dresser, the bedside tables, Dad's bureau — all held evidence of her home care. Pills. Vials. Needles. Kleenex. Bottles of Ensure.

"Did the nurse come today?" Why did I ask that? The silver pot the VONs used to sterilize tools for cleaning bedsores was sitting in the kitchen sink.

"Barbara, again. Mary-Jo tomorrow." Mom lifted her knees and pushed down the sheepskin blanket beneath her. I leaned in to help.

"You used to do that," I said.

"VON? Yes, after graduating from nursing school."

"Why VON?"

"Victorian Order of Nurses."

"Queen Victoria?"

She nodded. "Created as a gift to the queen, oh, a long, *long* time ago." She sipped from her straw and made a gurgling sound.

"I'll get more," I said, taking the plastic cup.

"Thanks, honey." She held my gaze. I let her hold it. I felt it then, that quality of being that people were drawn to, that light that grew from within, despite her body's deterioration. It flowed through me, through us. The unexpressed confidence she had in me.

"Tell me again, Mom, how you used to fight with the rocks."

"Oh, that." She smiled and grabbed hold of her Benson & Hedges, opened the pack.

Don't smoke! I wanted to yell but remembered Dad's words: *Leave your mother alone. It's one of the few pleasures she has left.*

"I haven't thought about that in years," said Mom.

"It wasn't that long ago you were telling Eleanor." Then again, maybe it was. I wanted a black Speedo that day and came home with a white cotton nightgown.

She lit a cigarette with her Zippo lighter and took a long drag before exhaling. "We did that when we were kids, when we were mad at each other. Collected rocks and piled them on the lawn of the person we were mad at. Seems funny now."

"The Quarrel Game," said Nana, standing by the bedroom door.

"Yes. You named it that, Mother. I'd forgotten."

"Quarrel. Like quarry," I said.

"Quarrel is an angry dispute, a squabble," said Nana. "Quarry is game, an animal pursued."

Quarry is outside our windows and inside this room — the open-aired bedsores. Quarrel *is me telling you to shut up.* "I'll be back with your water, Mom."

THE NEXT DAY after I'd parked the Malibu in the lot of the Niagara Clifton Motor Inn like I always did, Louie stepped down from the veranda and told me to get back in the car.

"I'm taking you to a new location. Motel up The Hill has an opening. We'll try you out there. Follow me," he said, jiggling his car keys.

Is that what Ted meant by "move you"?

I watched for Louie's Town Car in the rear-view mirror. Long and sleek, it made me think of the carp at the bottom of the quarry, the bottom feeders. I reversed the car when he drove past and followed him across the busy sidewalk, through the crowd of mingling tourists.

"Taking her to Canuck now," Louie shouted as he drove by Ted's booth.

Ted grinned. He was counting his wad of cash.

"Go get 'em, kid," he said, giving me a thumbs-up.

We'd barely driven up The Hill when traffic stopped for a passing freight train. Nothing to do but wait. I watched the tourists in the rear-view mirror. I could see my old booth, empty. When I looked again a moment later, Ted was standing behind it.

"Fucking Ted," I muttered.

When we arrived at the motel, I parked beside Louie and stepped out of the car. Louie pointed to my new booth, located beneath the Canuck Motel carport, not far from the motel office. "Pakis own the place. Come and meet Amir, the owner." I turned to Louie when he said that word — it wasn't right. He didn't notice my disapproval. He opened the lobby door. "Ladies first." When we entered the air-conditioned lobby, the sweat on my arms spiked to goosebumps.

"Where's your Daddy-O?" Louie said to the man standing behind the front desk.

At first I thought the man was a lot older than me but then I realized that his crisp white shirt and thin black tie that made him appear older, the white of his shirt made his skin look darker.

"He's at Impala today. We need a booth there, too," he said, eyeing my body.

I crossed my arms.

"This what you're giving us?"

"Caitlin, Shyam. Shyam, Caitlin."

Neither of us extended a hand. We were immersed in silence when the phone rang.

"Yeah, we got nice rooms. You want one for two nights? Stay three and we'll give you a special." Shyam quoted the rate. This ended the conversation.

"Harder to make a deal on the phone," he said to Louie, not me. "We need more walk-ins. How's The Hill today? Busy?"

"A bit slow. But things pick up. Long weekend around the corner. You booked for it?"

"Few Jacuzzi rooms left. Ever seen a heart-shaped bed, Caitlin?"

"She's not new at this," said Louie. He nudged the crook of my elbow. I could feel my face warming with embarrassment.

"Of course," said Shyam, his dark eyes steady. "She looks like an ol' pro." He laughed.

My insides squirmed.

"I'M NOT MAKING MONEY, Dad." I was dangling my toes above the quarry. A gather of sunfish rose to the fake bait. When I dunked my toes in, they nibbled.

"You need a new strategy. Think about it. You sold a few, you'll sell more. You want to go back to The Hill?"

"No. I hate The Hill." The clipboard approach had worked, but it was hard talking to strangers, despite the seller's high.

When he stood up from his lounger and started walking, the wooden dock beams vibrated to his pace. "I'm going in the house if you're not going in." He flipped through his file of work papers.

"What?"

"For God's sake, go back to Hideaway then."

"You mean... I don't have to do this anymore?"

He stuffed the papers back into the manila folder.

"She's having a bad day. I don't have time for this. Goddamn Florence. Moved my files again. Can't find a goddamn thing after her cleaning sprees. Are you going in or not?"

He was wearing another new T-shirt. The insignia brought to mind the scent of Polo aftershave. I thought of the comment Nana had made after I'd finally coaxed him off the office phone to watch me swim my lengths: "Aren't you looking sharp? Another night out?"

Dad dropped his folder onto the dock bench and checked his watch. "I've got a ball game to go to. Well?"

The water rippled where my toes had been. No food, the sunfish must've said to each other after their hopeful frenzy.

"I'll call Hideaway then. Tell them I'm available." I picked up my towel. "You look nice, Dad."

The tenseness on his face softened. "Change the look and you change the man."

But I didn't call Hideaway. I couldn't go back there. I couldn't face Darren, and Dad knew that.

I SAT BESIDE my new booth in a plastic chair shaped like a tilted flying saucer. I'd pulled it from the motel pool. *Swim at your own risk. Motel not responsible. No Lifeguard. Pool Unmanned.*

Unwomaned, I thought as I waited for tourists to walk by me.

This is how it usually went: tired and overheated from their drives across the States or Canada, the wife/mother waited in the car while the husband/father checked in. Whiny kids rushed out from the back seat to stretch, and when they saw the booth with the colourful photos, they ran to it.

"Look!" they squealed when they spotted the Spanish Aero Car. "Mom, can we do that?"

"I'll arrange for you to see these wonderful sights," I'd say. "A bus will pick you up, right here."

When Mom and her brood were interested, they leaned in. I had them. But then the husband/father would rush down the steps, wiggling the room key. "Get in the car. Room's around the back. I'll drive us over."

A man on a mission. A man with no interest in booking a bus tour.

"We'll be back," the wife/mother would say, avoiding my eyes.

One day a family did come back. "We went walking down that hill where all those funny museums are, and a nice man gave us a discount. He even arranged for the bus to pick us up here. He told us to wait by your booth."

When the bus – a green-painted school bus with no air conditioning, *our* tour bus – picked them up at *my* location, I cursed beneath my breath: "Fucking Ted."

A moment later a young couple appeared. "*Arrêtéz!*" they yelled in unison. But the green bus had already turned the corner.

"You have tickets?" I asked.

"*Oui,*" said the man. "We booked with you."

"Me?"

"Inside," said his wife, pointing to the office. She handed me the ticket.

I looked at the signature.

"That man at the desk," she said, taking back the ticket.

I was steaming now. Like the quarry in the early morning, when the sun extracts the night's cold. How dare Shyam sell tickets behind my back? The steam condensed behind my eyes. It didn't evaporate like I needed it to, to summon the courage to confront.

That evening when I arrived home, I heard the hum of Mom's sewing machine coming from the back bedroom where Nana slept. A warm glow moved through my anger. *The morphine must be working. She's having a good day.* But when I walked by the master bedroom on the way to my room, Mom was lying in the hospital bed, fast asleep. It was Nana on the sewing machine. My anger spiked.

I slipped on my black Speedo, went down to the dock and dove in. When I surfaced, I was touching a barrel. I'd finally made it to the floating raft, swimming underwater in one breath. *Yes, you did it.* Then the voice inside me said: *keep going, make it to the other side on your own.* I front-crawled past the raft and entered the rhythm of my limbs, made the calm water move to move me, made my mind rise like the body of the great blue heron, and when I looked down from above, I saw what I was: an arrow of swimming light.

THE FOLLOWING DAY I executed my new strategy. After each new couple or family checked in, I asked Shyam for their room number. I made note of where they parked and surreptitiously watched them unpack. After their door was shut, I listened for the muffled sound of a TV sitcom or the mechanical hum of the air conditioner, sounds that soothed their travel-weary souls.

Then, I knocked.

"Hi. I'm from the motel. My name is Caitlin. I'm here to tell you about our wonderful bus tour." I checked their eyes for interest and watched for leaning bodies. If they scoffed at the price — *that much?* — I informed them of today's special rate. "But you must book now. Our bus is filling up fast."

That night on the dock, I told Dad the news. "I filled half a bus, all on my own."

He gave me a high-five. "That a girl!" he said. "I knew you could do it." He checked his watch. "We'll tell your mother when she wakes up. Visits to the doctor tire her out." He sipped his Labatt's as he paced the dock.

I slipped into his lounger.

After a long stretch of silent pacing, he told me to turn around. "Too pale," he said, grabbing the bottle of QT. He squirted a dollop onto his hand and started spreading it over my shoulders and back. "This'll give you colour."

A FEW NIGHTS LATER, I was in the middle of a dream when I heard soft moans through my bedroom wall. "Caitlin, the pillow... my pillow fell..." Mom was alone. Dad was in Montreal on a business trip. Nana was asleep in the back bedroom. I didn't want to get up. In my dream, a handsome man — a cross between Michael Landon and Donny Osmond — was leaning in to kiss me. *No, don't pull me away from this...*

The Royal Connaught

"THERE SHE IS," he said when he saw me step off the elevator at Brandon Hall, the all-girls residence I lived in. He scanned my outfit from head to toe. I was wearing a blue dress underneath my navy peacoat, blue like the quarry on cold fall days.

Dad looked dapper standing there in his camel coat, elbows hooked on the front desk counter, ivory scarf looped around his neck. I thought of what he often said: *Change the look and you change the man.* The silk sheen brought out his post-summer tan. QT and sun. Dad's winning combination. Dark suit. Paisley tie. Strangers thought he was an actor — *Don't I know you from somewhere?* Seeing him standing there in the purple lobby, I understood why. He put out his arm. I slipped my arm through it. The desk ladies chittered as he led me out.

A valet at The Royal Connaught parked Dad's Caddy. I'd never seen a valet before, so I didn't understand why we'd need one. Until I stepped out. The October wind and sudden rain blew fiercely across my face and up the skirt of my knee-length dress. It shot through the cuffs of my peacoat, a coat Dad always admired. "I had one just like that growing up," he said whenever he saw me wearing it.

We entered the lobby. Gold and deep burgundies signalled: *this place has class.* Wainscotting and high ceilings and crystal chandeliers. No greasy cafeteria food for me tonight. I thought of the envy on my roommate's face while I waited for Dad's arrival. "Lucky you," Suzie had said, grabbing hold of her food card. "I get to eat crap tonight."

"Dad... this place."

He smiled and squeezed my hand.

"Maharg," he said to the elegant hostess, whose auburn hair was set in one perfect wave.

We followed her to a corner table. Patrons watched Dad as we weaved through the crowded room.

"What are you doing?" I whispered to Dad. He'd cut in front of my red velvet chair. When he pulled it out from the table, I understood. He was being a gentleman. Even Nana would be proud.

A moment later our waiter came by with a silver jug. He fanned the linen napkins onto our laps and filled our water glasses. We opened the heavy menus.

"Well," Dad said, putting the big menu down to read the little one. "This *is* a special occasion. Nineteen. It's official. I'd like to buy your first drink."

He was beaming when he said that. I smiled to hide my truth. This wouldn't be my first, but one of many. Sipping

Mom's rye and ginger when she wasn't looking, downing a mouthful of Dad's Labatt's, guzzling warm beer at keg parties at Hideaway with Darren. Drinking gave the feeling of floating, of being away from the worries in my stomach.

"What will it be?" He handed me the cocktail list.

Pink lady. Tequila sunrise. Piña colada. Pretty, feminine names. I didn't want pretty. I wanted harsh. I closed the menu. "Black Russian."

He probably wanted to say *are you sure?* But he held his tongue and nodded. "Good choice. I'll have one, too."

When the squat glasses arrived, he made a toast. "To your first," he said, winking. He clinked my raised glass.

Of course he knew. How *could* this be my first? But it was my first drink with my father on the right side of the law.

It burned going down. I'd taken in too much.

"You okay?" he said, watching me cough.

"Fine." I sipped some water.

"Kahlúa. Vodka. You might try a brown cow next time, a little milk to soften the blow."

I made myself finish it. Not as fast as Dad finished his, but my cocktail was gone by the time our entrées arrived under silver domes. Their lids were removed and taken from the table.

"She wanted to be here," he said. "She asked me to give you this."

I took the pink bag from his reach across the table and set it beside my steaming dinner. I didn't wait to open it. I dug through the folds of white tissue. "A bride mouse?" I said, holding her up. The memory of my cousin Cindy came back to me: *My parents have wedding photos. Yours don't have any.* Why would Mom give me this?

Nobody at university knew I had a mother with cancer, not even Suzie. I could pretend things were normal at home, that Mom wasn't getting worse. I could forget the hospital bed in the master bedroom, the VON visits, the commode, the stench from bedsores, the fights between Nana and Dad, Mom's shrinking form. Instead I told Suzie how my parents were born with the same surname. "Cool!" she'd said. "It's like fate, their meeting each other. How rare is that?"

Would Suzie think my wedding mouse was childish? So what if she did?

"Careful," said Dad. "Don't get your supper on it."

Dinner, Nana would say, scolding him.

"I won't," I said, setting the mouse on my lap. Her whiskers tickled my inner wrist, and her button nose was cold on my palm. Her eyes didn't click shut like the eyes of the two antique porcelain dolls at home – they remained wide open. "She's so much bigger than the Quarry Craft mice Mom makes. Her gown's beautiful."

"One of a kind," Dad said as if he'd made her. "Sewn especially for you. Come on," he said, wiping an eye. "Our dinners are getting cold."

I didn't want to disappoint Dad, so I forced myself to eat all the trout. When the waiter removed our empty plates, Dad reached inside his jacket pocket. There was something tucked in the palm of his hand. I couldn't get a glimpse.

"Some nineteen years ago I took your mother to this place. If memory serves me right, we sat at this same table. She wore blue like you – funny how that happens." He looked into my eyes. "It was here at The Royal Connaught I asked your mother to marry me." On the flat of his hand, a red felt box. "Here," he said. "Open it."

I did and the candlelight veined the glimmering opal into a broken rainbow. "It's beautiful, Dad."

He leaned forward. "Put it on."

The only finger it fit was the ring finger – tight like a slipper on a foot.

"*Mom, why don't we have any wedding photos of you and Dad?*"

"*Your father and I wanted to keep things simple,*" she'd said, combing the damp tangles from my freshly washed hair. "*It made sense to elope.*"

I remember thinking *how romantic* when she told me this. But now I thought: *wouldn't she miss wearing a white wedding dress? You don't wear a gown to elope.*

I WAS GETTING READY TO GO and study in the library. I gathered my books and looked out the dorm room window. December snow was starting to fall. The telephone rang.

"It's for you," said Suzie. She passed me the receiver.

"Hello?"

"Pack your things. You're coming home. Your mom's in the hospital and it doesn't look good. Goddamn Nana, taking her to Buffalo to Christmas shop. Out in the damn cold – pneumonia... what was she thinking?"

Three in a Room

SHE DIED CHRISTMAS DAY. I knew she would. A voice had told me. A voice that wasn't mine but must've been. None of this made sense. But sometimes it did, when I tried not to think about it. Like the way you see a star by looking to the left, just a little.

The quarry was cold when she went into the hospital for the last time, but not cold enough to form a skin. It received the snow and turned the snow to water. Eventually, it would scab over, cap the quarry of life. The fish would anchor rock bottom, dormant in their crypt.

Mom said strange things those last few days while I sat by her bedside in her private room, flipping through old magazines. She seemed anxious about someone. The name Geordie passed through her morphined mouth, followed by: *don't ... stop it.*

I touched her arm. "Who's Geordie, Mom?"

She muttered more nonsense.

Still, I thought, she'll come through. She always did. I thought of the time (two years ago? three?) when she spat out blood. I'd never seen such vile red. Even that time she'd come through.

I never knew you could lose so much in one day. And on the biggest day of giving, the day set aside to open gifts with loved ones. I should've gone to the hospital; I'd heard the voice by then: *She'll die on Christmas Day.* But Dad's shift was first, and his Caddy was already gone by the time I woke up.

I was watching an old episode of *Little House on the Prairie* in the family room. The horse-drawn covered wagon was trundling across the television screen when I heard the side door open. He came straight through without taking off his boots. He stood in the middle of the family room for what seemed like a long time. Long enough for the snow to slide off and form a blurry puddle.

"She's gone."

"I know."

Round and round. And then the world stopped.

I'D NEVER BEEN TO A visitation before. It seemed silly calling it that, especially when the person you're visiting isn't there to receive you. Was her spirit in the red gladioli crowning her glossy coffin, or perhaps in the blue-ribboned word *Mother*?

That was the day I devised a no-tear strategy. Crying drained, and I needed the energy. Nineteen and no mother. When Reverend Barker began his eulogy — *yes, he really is talking about her in the past tense* — I sang the alphabet song in my head: *A-B-C-D...* I let the letters roll through: *X-Y-Z.* For all I knew, my lips could've been moving. But that sight would be permissible in a stained-glass windowed church with cold December light cutting through. I'd look like I was praying.

"Thanks be to God," said Reverend Barker.

I didn't want to thank God. I wanted to tell him to fuck off. But what if there really were a Heaven and my curse prevented Mom from entering the gates? She died on Christmas Day, His son's birthday.

What happened next startled me. I shut my eyes to stop the sensation. *See her cratered bedsores—fleshy, blistered potholes on hip and tailbone, the insides yellow, crusty, mushy.* When I put my hand on the smooth oak pew, Dad squeezed it. Tears flowed from his eyes. I took a deep breath. The urge to laugh had stopped.

I stared at the coffin at the front of the church. *She's not in there.*

Nana had insisted on an open coffin. "It's how death's done," she'd said to Dad in the hallway of Thompson's Funeral Home.

Dad looked at me beside him in my old black skirt and my new blue sweater. A sweater Mom had given me, her last Christmas gift to me, the gift I'd opened that morning, dreamily stunned. A monogrammed sweater she'd bought in Buffalo when Nana had taken her out Christmas shopping. Mid-December. Dad away at a sales convention. Me away at university. No one there to say: *no, no, no.*

Did Nana feel any guilt? Because of the pneumonia, Mom's wish to die at home beside her beloved quarry didn't happen.

I thought back to that first time we saw it, the look of calm on my mother's face, how Dad thought the quarry would heal her.

Before the funeral, all Nana talked about was the open coffin. "She needs to see the body for closure, Donald." She sucked her gold tooth, her eyes unblinking. "You'll regret this."

But Dad didn't want me to remember her as sick. He didn't want cancer's decay to be the last vision of my mother.

BETWEEN THE VISITATION and the funeral, Nana spent her time cleaning the bungalow. She dusted knick-knacks, mopped the peg-wood floor, wiped the ceiling's corners for cobwebs that weren't there. The smell of ammonia pinched my nose. "A new broom sweeps clean," she said when I dodged past her dust piles. "But an old one knows the corners."

The night of the funeral, Dad came to my room.

"You okay?" he said.

I dog-eared *King Lear* and closed the paperback. I'd been exempt from Christmas exams, but I had so much work to catch up on.

"Mom said weird things in the hospital. She seemed upset."

"Your mother? That was the morphine talking, the coma she was in from the goddamn pneumonia." He pushed my legs to the side with the sweep of his hand and sat down at the edge of my bed. "Listen. Florence wants those dishes back, those bird willows."

"Blue Willows?"

"Your mother had to deal with her silent treatment growing up but not me. She doesn't want to talk? Fine. Yes, the Blue Willows *and* the dolls. The day of her daughter's funeral." He shook his head.

Mom loved those dolls. One dressed in blue, the other in pink. One brunette, the other blonde. Matching hats, kid-leather gloves and black leather booties. Attached to metal stands, they sat where Mom could easily see them whenever she wanted to, when she wasn't sewing or smoking or looking out at the quarry. The dolls' blue eyes were always open, ready to receive her thoughtful stares.

Dad looked pale sitting there. When did he get so pale?

"She's not getting them." He was looking at me now. He was waiting for me to say something, as if he'd just given a sales pitch and was waiting for the prospective client's response.

"Are you sure Nana wants them? Aren't they Mom's now?"

"Think about it. Think about the message she's giving us."

"When did she say this?"

"What's that got to do with it?" He stood up to deal with his agitation. He paced the aisle between the twin beds. "Shh. She's coming down the hall."

We listened to the click of her heels.

"Night, Florence," said Dad.

THE NEXT MORNING Nana left for Owen Sound. She drove all the way back to her two-storey red brick house, the house Mom had grown up in, where Nana lived her structured life – curling in winter, golfing in summer, delivering for Meals on Wheels, singing in the St. Andrew's Presbyterian Church choir, praying to God.

She was gone when I woke up. So were the dolls and the dishes.

Dad didn't mention the dolls or the dishes. I waited all day for him to mention them. I waited the next day, too. And then the waiting grew into stone and the stone formed a wall.

He placed Mom's tennis trophies where the dolls once sat. They filled the shelves that held the Maharg silence.

I'D COME BACK TO the quarry for the weekend after starting my second year of my psychology degree. Suzie had wanted me to stay on campus to attend a house party with her, but Dad wanted me home. We sat at the gate-leg table eating cold take-out pizza. Mom would have made us reheat it. The pizza was cheesy and spongy, the way Dad liked it.

"This Christmas we're going to New York City," he said, chewing.

I put down my slice. "*Christmas?* It's only September. And I've been to New York. Grade twelve, remember?" With so many places in the world to visit, why would I want to go somewhere twice?

"But Caitlin, *we've* never been."

I nodded then as I'd been nodding numbly for the past year, my chin heavy from all that grief. I looked at Dad sitting there, chewing — his eyes were rimmed with dark circles, his wrinkles, deeper.

THERE WERE STAINS on the luggage where the snow had melted. Little trails of tears. Dad yanked back the floor-length curtains. He craned his neck to look up. I did the same. I knew then why they called them skyscrapers. We were alone in a city, the city of layers, under layers of snow. We were at the St. Regis Hotel in a room with two double beds, just me and my father.

I ran my hand across a pillow — smooth and silky, delicate yet thick. Mom would've known the thread count. "You sure we can afford this?"

"Fellow who first owned this, a guy named Astor, drowned in the sinking Titanic. But what a monument he left." Dad extended his arms. "Of course we can afford it! Relax! You sound like your Nana." He shook his hips like Elvis. "We're in the Big Apple, baby!"

"Dad!" My face warmed. Even with no one around, I couldn't help but feel embarrassed by my father. Yet also pleased, the way I used to feel when I was a little girl. He grinned proudly.

CHRISTMAS DAY, at the New York deli, the room smelled of kielbasa and vinegar. If I fingered the air, I could catch grease, but there was enough congealing on my plate. I couldn't fit my mouth around the club sandwich, so I took small bites. Dad talked with his mouth full. The mustard on his upper lip matched his v-neck sweater. I knew who'd given him that v-neck sweater.

Linda.

"There's someone I want you to meet," Dad had said during one of our biweekly phone calls.

"Who?"

"You have lots in common."

"Who, Dad?"

He called her "a friend." A week later, when he phoned my dorm room, he called her "a good friend."

I rolled my eyes.

When I first met Linda, Mom had been dead for five months and not long buried. Linda was sitting next to my father when I arrived at the restaurant. The booth in the Fort Erie Steakhouse held the shape of a half-circle. When I settled down on the plush seat, I locked Dad in the middle.

Her hair was blonde (not red), her eyes green (not blue), her skin pale (no freckles), her teeth straight (no front-tooth gap), but when she stood up to shake my hand, she was Mom's height.

One good thing the chemo did for Mom was smooth her skin. No wrinkles. Not even where the bone-pain gathered. Her face looked younger as the years pushed her forward, except for the red squiggles congregating around her nose. Rosacea. The name of a flower. But even with such smooth skin, she never looked as young as the blonde nestled next to my father.

Small talk. So small the talk turned invisible. Until – "You've things in common," Dad said, looking at me. "Linda's studying psychology."

"An M.A.?"

"No. B.A. like you, but part-time." He'd said it before Linda had the chance to. "All that primary-school teaching keeps you busy, right?" He touched her arm.

When she nodded, her bangs vibrated. She had straight hair. I'd always wanted straight hair.

There was so much there on our plates that first meeting in the candle-lit restaurant, we could've talked about anything: psychology, the sirloin steaks, the Merlot, the garlic bread, the way spring appears full force overnight, all those blossoms opening, opening the age gap between them, the gap missing from her teeth, the gap I missed, the gap in me.

Amazing how many people ate deli sandwiches on Christmas Day. No tables available and the line by the door kept on growing. It was nice to sit and feel warm again, though my hands were cold. They were always cold.

Dad was telling me a story he'd never told before, about his and Mom's first Christmas together, when they were living in Hamilton, in an apartment on the Niagara Escarpment. What Hamiltonians called "the mountain," though it wasn't a mountain.

"They had nowhere to go, the young fellows. Young as you, maybe younger, so I said to the two of them, there on the street, day before Christmas, 'Come to our place tomorrow, we'll give you a warm supper.'"

"What did Mom say?"

He put down his smoked-meat sandwich and wiped the mustard off his upper lip. "She said, 'Good thing we bought a big turkey. We'll be ready if they do come by.'"

"And did they?"

He chewed his last bite and nodded.

"Why did you do it? They were strangers."

"Before my luck changed and I met your mother, a family did the same for me once. And when I asked how I could repay them, they told me – do the same for someone else."

On the snowy walk back to the hotel, I wondered why he'd never told me that before. I wondered how many other things he had to tell me. How many things Mom never got the chance to tell me. But would she have? Still waters run deep. What people said about her quiet nature. What had lived beneath those still waters?

As we ascended the red-carpeted steps of our hotel, the doorman, dressed in a top hat and tails, greeted us like he greeted the people after us. He remembered our names, but we would not be remembered.

When Dad opened the door to our hotel room, I saw a blinking red light.

"We have a message," he said, acting surprised. He flicked the light switch.

I stepped into the bathroom. A paper strip lay across the toilet lid. *Clean and fresh.* I crumpled it into a ball. After flushing, I heard his voice. He was talking to someone he knew well. When I opened the door, he put down the phone. He stood there staring at my double bed.

"What?" I said.

He sat on his bed and nodded for me to sit.

"That was Linda. She's having a tough time this Christmas. She's booked a flight. She'll be here tomorrow."

"Here? What do you mean, here?"

"You heard what I said." He pointed to my bed. "There's enough room." He stood up and removed his yellow sweater. It landed beside me. "After I shower, we'll head out. You want to see the figure skaters, don't you?"

The click of the bathroom door.

I glared at the yellow. I threw it on his bed.

THAT FIRST WINTER at the quarry when the water froze over and the ice grew thick enough to carry our weight, the three of us went out skating. The blistering wind had swept much of the snow off the surface. I'd never skated outdoors before, only inside the cold, dry Grimsby arena, where I circled counter-clockwise until my ankles tired or I slipped and fell.

Once we made our way off the dock and onto the ice, we didn't have to circle around. We could go anywhere in any direction. The grey ice gleamed. Off we went in search of the smoothest strips, for the winter weather had pimpled some patches of ice. When we found the smooth parts, we sped up to glide, extended our arms like the wings of water birds.

One time Mom and I heard a guttural *glub, glub* followed by an extended *crackle*. We froze to listen.

"It's safe, remember?" Dad had said. Despite his deep-seated fear of water, he had no fear on ice.

THERE WERE LITTLE JAM JARS on our breakfast table. Marmalade and strawberry. No plastic packets in this fancy place. The jars were sealed with paper strips. *Fresh and clean,* they read. Dad wasn't talking with his mouth full this morning. He kept shifting in his chair. The hotel restaurant was nearly empty; most tables had already been reset with sealed jars.

I couldn't finish my toast, so Dad ate it for me. While waiting for him to finish, I picked up a jar and read the fine print: *Not for individual sale.*

"Take it."

"What?"

"Take the damn thing." He grabbed it from my hand and put it in his jacket pocket.

"But I don't want yellow."

He put it back and pocketed the red.

The red light was blinking again when we got back to the room. I stepped into the bathroom and squirted toothpaste on my toothbrush. When I grabbed for a towel, he was standing by the bathroom door.

"Jesus, Dad. You scared me."

"She's here. She's on her way. We'll meet her in the lobby." He scanned the bathroom. "We'll need more towels," he said, rubbing his chin. "I need a quick shave."

In the marble lobby, two high-backed chairs that faced the front desk were free, so that's where we sat. The white-shirted employees behind the desk went through stages of busy, calm, busy. I wondered what I'd look like in a white pressed shirt and name tag, my name engraved in gold, gold like the gleaming lobby. *Caitlin. Here to serve you.* The tag wouldn't say that, but that's what it would mean.

Dad's knee pumped like a jackhammer.

I turned to the elevators. Couples and families getting on and off, carrying shopping bags. Boxing Day. Then I remembered — they didn't call it that here.

The winter earth, post-Christmas, had been too cold to receive her coffined body. We had to wait for spring's slow thaw. They'd housed her in the Greenwood Cemetery mausoleum, a crypt-like limestone monstrosity of a building, for the Owen Sound winter, and it was during those months I began to have nightmares that she wasn't dead. She was asleep like Snow White in her long glass coffin, only the coffin wasn't glass, it was oak. And the body inside the open coffin wasn't pretty. The skin was yellowed with pus, black where the boils had cracked, caked red where the dead blood had gathered, the stench of fish rot.

One night at a campus bar, the vision shot through me. I tried to destroy it by downing Long Island iced tea, the strongest drink I could think of, but the alcoholic concoction only fuelled the horror. Up she sat in her open coffin. She grabbed for my hand.

"She's here," said Dad.

By the time I turned in the high-backed chair, Linda had already stepped through the St. Regis entrance into the lobby.

IT WAS HARD WALKING in twos down the frantic sidewalks of Manhattan, so threes were close to impossible. Bags and elbows and bustling bodies. Snow in your face. But I was getting used to the squawking honks from the parade of yellow taxis and the awkward silence between us all.

Dad looked at the street sign. "This way," he said.

Gold doors and high-fashion mannequins. A crowd had gathered by the model in the window, who was trying not to blink. I stared at her nose, where air moved in and out.

Dad tugged the sleeve of my peacoat. "Come on. We're going inside."

The department store was so long I couldn't see the end of it. Coiffed women stationed like sentinels. Bottles in hand, ready to spray.

I scanned the nearby shelves for a bottle of Chanel No. 5 and sprayed some on my wrist. *Now you will smell her.* Not the cancer-ridden bedsore smell that permeated my nightmares, but the scent of a healthy mother. I sniffed. Something was missing. Oils—hers—to make the mother scent.

Linda exposed her wrist to a sprayer. Dad sniffed. "What do you think?" he said, looking at me.

I knew the fruity scent from a girl in residence, an annoying, chatty friend of my roommate Suzie. I didn't like the scent then, so I knew I wouldn't like it now. "It doesn't work for me," I said, stuffing my hands in my coat pockets.

"Not for you. Here." He grabbed Linda's wrist and led it to my face.

When I tried not to smell it, I sneezed. "Oops," I said, and wiped my nose. I'd drizzled snot on her inner wrist.

"It's okay," said Linda, grabbing a Kleenex from her purse.

"Jesus," said Dad. "Enough of this." He undid the knot

in his plaid scarf. "You wanna look at clothes, you look at clothes."

So we split up. Dad went to the Men's. Linda and me, the Ladies'.

"Caitlin?"

The tap on my arm made me jump. Linda was holding something, something yellow. "You okay? I thought this sweater would look pretty on you."

I didn't want to try it on but I did. I don't know why. Shades of yellow washed me out.

WE HAD SPEARS in our hands. Long silver sticks. We stabbed the bread cubes and dunked them into the bubbling cheese, gathered our lift in cheesy strings. The fondue restaurant had been Linda's suggestion. We'd left the travel guide at the hotel and were too tired and hungry to get it.

"You're not eating anymore, Caitlin," said Dad.

I stabbed the smallest chunk of bread and swirled it above the bubbling cheese. "See?"

"That's not eating. That's playing with your goddamn food."

Linda smiled at me. "Maybe she's not that hungry, Don. Did I pick the wrong place?"

"We'd have fainted by now if you hadn't spotted it. It's New York City. We do new things."

I never thought to ask Linda why she'd come to New York or why she was having a tough time that Christmas. I couldn't direct my thoughts to outcomes. They melted like snow on the tongue.

I had extra space on the long wooden bench, sitting across from Dad and Linda. They were probably touching knees. So

I guess Linda was smart to choose a place like Swiss Bliss. We didn't have to stare at each other. We could stare at the pot and respond after swallows with *yum, um* and other guttural noises. And when that died down, we could listen to the voices around us. The little girl sitting next to me didn't want to stab her bread with cheese.

"Chocolate. I want chocolate."

"You'll get chocolate," said a woman in a black dress. "But you have to eat the cheese first."

The little girl put down her stick and crossed her arms. She started kicking the bench with the back of her foot. *Thunk. Thunk.* I could feel the vibrations. Like a ticking clock, and I hated the sound of a ticking clock, like Nana's grandfather clock that sat in her kitchen in Owen Sound. It took away your concentration, and that's what her foot was doing. *Thunk. Thunk.* Taking a piece of me I didn't want to give. I slid my foot over to block her swing. She stopped. She didn't look at me. She was looking at the waitress carrying a pot of her precious chocolate.

Maybe grief was more like snow, falling and falling, taking the shape of your body. There must be some way to make peace, for grief to live on but less heavy. Snow melts to water, water lets you float.

The little girl was eating her lip-smacking chocolate. She looked at the liquid she'd pooled around her fork before tonguing the nutty layer. Eyes half shut. She made this sound like she was sucking a soother, her tongue tapping the roof of her mouth. Horrible, that little slap. I slid down the bench as far as I could without touching the knee of the next stranger, but the little smack followed. I couldn't get away from it. And when I closed my eyes, I felt this slap inside me. The sound of dirt hitting wood, of dirt flying from shovels. I shifted back beside the girl in one long swoop and tipped her milk onto her lap.

"Mommy!"

I righted the glass and used my serviette to stop the dripping. "Sorry," I said.

"It's okay, honey. Accidents happen."

I smiled when I heard that voice, the tone maternal. But when I looked up to say thank you, the woman was leaning toward her daughter.

WE WALKED BACK to the hotel carrying our brown bags of stuff. American flags flapped in the wind. We didn't have so many flags back home. Only on Canada Day. Here every day was America Day. Red, white and blue. Except for blue we had the other colours. What made theirs so bold? Stars and stripes versus the hand of a leaf. That's what it looked like, the palm of a hand in the shape of a leaf. My palm in a plaster of Paris when I was in Grade one. Once the imprint hardened, I brought it home.

"I love it," Mom had said, placing her palm on the imprint, her hand healthy and big. Her palm didn't fit but that wasn't the point. The point was to press herself in, the way I'd pressed myself in, to make a mark out of me.

I hadn't had any wine at Swiss Bliss, but when we stepped into the hotel lobby, I wished I had. Our daytime adventure was over. Next step—sleep. Me and Linda in the same double bed.

"How about a nightcap?" I said, peering into the lobby bar, home of the Bloody Mary, the red snapper.

Dad headed toward the elevators, but Linda stepped back.

"I see a saxophone. Must be live music. A nightcap would be nice. Don?"

In the lounge Dad sat next to me, Linda across the table. We ordered some draughts. The waitress carried them over on a round tray. She set down three beer mats, then three beers. We all looked at the beers.

"Wait," Dad said. The waitress turned. "They're foam-heavy."

"Pardon me?"

"You heard me." He held one up. "It's half foam."

"Don," said Linda, "they're not that bad."

Dad hit the drinks menu. "For what they're charging in here?"

"Sir, I'd be happy to return these for you, sir." The waitress righted her round tray.

"I've already sipped mine," I said, rubbing lip gloss from the rim.

He pulled the pint from my hand and passed it to the puzzled waitress. He did it so quickly, it nearly toppled. "Here," said Dad.

"Oh," she said in a different voice, high and thin. She wiped her fingers on the front of her black skirt. "I'll be back in a moment."

With no beers to look at, we looked at Dad's drumming fingers.

"They were bad," he said. "I know my beer."

Linda's chin tilted upwards. It looked like she wanted to say something. When her lips parted, I thought, *here it comes*, but the sound was a dry cough.

I stared at the barroom wall, the mural of Old King Cole.

"See his face?" Dad said. We looked at the king's face.

"He's letting one go."

"No," said Linda.

"Oh, yeah," Dad said. He lifted his leg and tilted the chair.

"Don," said Linda.

"Dad!" I said.

He mimicked the king's grin. "Look at the two of you." He laughed. "You look like them." Dad slapped his knee as he eyed the others in the mural. "See?"

Sure enough, the jesters were laughing, the pageboys blanching and the knights covering their mouths. The king's feet were twisted like his face.

A different waitress brought our beers. Her dark hair was streaked with a grey strip, like a lopsided skunk. She didn't look at us when she set down the glasses.

No foam. Only the odd floating bubble.

Three songs later, the three of us sat facing the same direction like sparrows turned toward the sun. As if the sax, the sound of the sun, had unravelled the knots in our bodies, the fresh tension we'd brought to the table and passed on to the waitress, the one who never came back.

We thought they were finished, the trio, so when the skunk-haired waitress whizzed by us again, Dad asked for the bill. We gathered our bags and our coats. With our backs to the musicians, we weren't prepared for another song.

Perhaps I should say I wasn't. When the music started, my body tightened. I turned to Dad. He was watching them play their song – his and my mother's, "This Guy's in Love With You." Did Linda know? I checked her expression. It seemed she'd picked up on something.

"Don?" she said, looking at the floor. "Your scarf."

I'd seen his eyes do that. Retreat and push at the same time. Only this time he wasn't looking at the family room floor.

It's a beautiful song, a hard one to play, and the trio played it well. No vocalist. It could've been worse. Linda picked up the scarf and wrapped it around his neck and set green bills on the table. After Dad blinked, his gaze resettled. But for that brief moment, he'd shown more control than that model we saw in the Fifth Avenue window. I didn't see his chest move.

WE TOOK TURNS doing our nightly ablutions, our end-of-the-day wash, rinse and spit. *Time for your ablutions,* Mom used to say, an expression she learned from Nana and passed down to me.

"You go first, Caitlin," said Dad.

This gave Dad and Linda some time alone. It made me think of that silly math puzzle – how to get the fox and the chickens across a river in three trips without the fox eating the chickens. Something like that. But no matter how hard I tried to figure the puzzle out, the fox always ate the chickens or the chickens drowned. They never made it to the other side.

Linda's bottles lined the back of the toilet. Her space. Dad's shaving kit in one corner of the counter. My make-up bag tucked in the other.

Aloe vera. Linda's ammo for good skin. I thought of the plant, smooth and rubbery green, thick and tough until a knife released the juice. I squirted a dollop on the back of my hand. Scent of rain, of green growing. It reminded me of the quarry when the ice first split. All those wet-buried smells seeping up and up.

Would Linda smell the aloe vera when I came out of the bathroom? I sniffed my hand. She might. I put my hand back under the tap. Their laughter carried through the wall. When I turned off the tap, their laughter stopped.

I'd made splashes on the mirror from shaking the water off my hand, so when I looked back at my reflection, it was scored with tears. People said I looked like Mom – *You have the same eyes – deep blue, deep set –* but I couldn't see it. I brushed the bangs from my forehead. They popped right back. They had more energy than my body.

We never did talk about the song the trio played. By the time Dad unlocked the door to our room, I knew that we wouldn't.

Crazy to think I would be sleeping with Linda.

As if I didn't know.

I had seen them naked already, last summer, the second summer I discovered I could sell like my father.

"See!" he'd said. "It's in your blood." Light trickled through his grieving eyes.

One slow August day, Louie told me to go home. "Take the afternoon off," he said after chatting with Shyam in the motel lobby.

Clear blue sunny sky. The quarry would be extra warm. I could rinse the tourist city from my pores.

When I entered the kitchen, I looked out the window. The water lay calm, inviting. Perfect for doing laps. It mirrored the evergreens and the edges of limestone. Even the floating raft was still.

"Hello?"

No answer. But Dad's car was in the carport. Was he on the dock? The dock, empty. He must be trimming hedges.

Fastidious. The new word for Dad. Before Mom's death, he was never tidy. He'd leave a messy trail through the house: socks on the chesterfield, tie on a chair, Rolaids on the counter. It drove Nana crazy.

"Keys? Where are my car keys?" he would say. He could never find them, so Mom and I bought him a key clapper. Clap your hands and the contraption answered: *Here I am.* Well, not quite like that, but it made a sound to home in on. Problem was, he lost that too.

I bypassed the family room and walked through the living room toward the bedrooms. No TV on. No radio. Dad didn't like it quiet. Where was the sound of his favourite radio station, The Music of Your Life? The big bands and the crooners like Bing and Sinatra. I wasn't supposed to swim alone, but a quick dip wouldn't hurt.

A creak and a moan. Did they come at once? Through the crack of the master bedroom door, I saw two naked bodies clasped like hands, rocking.

"Shit!"

Who said *shit* I don't remember. I was in my bedroom by then, sandwiched between the twin beds, my body stiff as the maple headboards.

I heard Dad's bedroom door click and the whoosh of running water, mumbles and moving around. I still hadn't moved by the time I heard his door creak open. Footsteps down the hall. A softer set followed. A moment later they were outside. I could see them through my bedroom window. Dad with his clippers. Linda holding the bushel basket. *Snip. Snip.* Down came unruly branches. Linda stooped to pick them up.

I slipped on my black Speedo and wrapped a beach towel around my waist.

"Hi, Dad," I said, walking toward them, the dry grass itchy on my feet.

He stopped snipping to look my way.

"Caitlin? What a surprise. What are you doing home so early?"

"I...it was a slow day. No check-ins. Louie told me to go home."

Linda twisted Dad's wrist toward her face. "Gosh, is that the time, Don? I'd better get going. I had no idea it was so late. Lovely to see you again, Caitlin." She was already walking briskly away when she said my name. She didn't look back.

I heard a motor start, so her car must've been there. She must've parked it on the other side of the carport.

"WHAT'S WITH ALL THE WATER on the mirror?" Dad said from the hotel bathroom, his voice relaxed from laughing with Linda.

Linda smiled when I shrugged. She fastened the top button of her flannel pajamas. I still had to change into mine, so I told Dad to stay in the bathroom until it was safe to come out. I felt weird with Linda there, even with the psych book propped on her lap. *Transactional Analysis.* Parent. Adult. Child. The trio in all of us. I wanted Linda to lift her book and tuck her head into it.

I didn't tell her I was a thrasher in sleep, that I tossed and turned and moled myself in. Even during the hot summer, I couldn't sleep without some kind of cover over me. A clam, a snail, a turtle. All blankets were mine during nightly journeys.

Dad came out wearing his blue pajamas. When Linda finished with her ablutions, he flicked on the TV. Joan Rivers had replaced a vacationing Johnny Carson and was attacking Madonna and her hairy armpits. That got the loudest laugh. With my Salvador Dali book on my lap, I stared at the melting clock on the cover. When I looked up to see why the audience was laughing, Rivers was clapping like a seal. She looked like one too, in her sleek black dress. Her hair, a flat tail of water.

What if time could melt? Is that what Dali believed? Melt and drip yet hang together, a river with hands? I grabbed the hotel pen on the bedside table and scribbled in the margin: *Melt and drip yet hang together, a river of hands. A hand of rivers, drip and melt yet together hang.* I drew a tornado beside it.

Linda peered over at my book. "Dali used to live here, one of the upper suites, I think. He and his wife." She flicked off her bedside lamp. "Good night, Don. Sweet dreams, Caitlin."

Dali, here? How did she know that? The guidebook, I guessed.

The melting clock stared back at me. Its face limp like laundry. Or perhaps stiff like laundry. Starched and bone-dry from the harsh beating of the sun. When I looked over at Dad, his eyes were closed. His hands folded neatly on his chest. Close to sleep or there already. His steady breath a contrast to Rivers' jerky motions.

Mom liked Joan Rivers. She was one of the few comedians who made Mom laugh. That soft smile brought to sound. I closed my eyes to remember. The laughter wouldn't come, so I reached for the remote. The screen blackened. I placed my hardcover book in the middle of the bed like a door stopper and flicked off the last light. I closed my eyes and waited for her voice. I waited some more. Nothing. I pushed my mind to the time we watched the hit movie *Ten*. That silly scene with Dudley Moore running up and down the Hollywood

Hills. He was trying to get back to his house to answer the phone, but he kept on falling and scrambling around like a lost rodent, was that it? His antics had made Mom laugh. I saw us in the family room, watching the video. I'd captured the visual but still no sound. I squeezed my eyes to turn up the volume. Nothing. I gave up on sound and examined the image. Her mouth curled. Her mouth opened.

When I opened my eyes, I heard breathing around me. How quickly they'd fallen asleep. I was in the middle of the moment I'd been dreading since Linda's arrival. No, before that. Since Dad had said, "She's having a tough time. She'll sleep in your bed."

But that's not exactly what he'd said. I wasn't remembering his words right. Why couldn't I remember things clearly anymore? I was melting like the clock, the book cover that separated me from Linda. But I was the clock on the book. I was the dead weight between them.

"Psychology. What are you going to do with that?" Dad had asked, repeatedly. With Linda studying it he'd stopped asking that question. I recalled the poster I'd taped to my dorm room wall, the big, fat bunny with long, droopy ears: *You're no bunny till some bunny loves you.*

Dad had Linda. Who was going to love me?

THE DREAM JABBED my cradle of sleep. Red jam all over Mom's face, red like the caked blood in the image from my nightmare. I swallowed my breath. *Where am I?* Then I remembered. I was in a New York hotel room between two sleeping people. I was far away from home.

Red jam all over her face. Stench of fish rot. The image seared.

I had to find that jam jar. Where did Dad put it? I got out of bed and turned on the bathroom light to help me see. I checked his pants pockets—just the clink of small change. I checked the dresser for the shape of a cylinder. I was past reason now, my mind all fetch. No jam jar here. None there. Coat pocket. Is that where Dad put it? I opened the closet door and felt for wool. Inside the pocket, the coolness of glass. I slipped into the bathroom and opened the lid—the sugary scent of fruit-squished things. I dipped in my finger and licked. I licked and licked and licked until the red was buried inside me.

I WAS SECOND IN LINE for morning ablutions. "Fox and chicken," I said out loud under the shower nozzle. When I picked up the small bar of soap, I saw a curly hair in the curve of the tub. *So she's not a real blonde.* I directed the spray over the dark evidence, watched it ricochet down the drain.

Turns out I didn't end up hogging the blankets. The Dali book had done the trick.

We were the last of the guests to eat breakfast at the hotel restaurant. When we finished eating, I pocketed a jar, a fresh one from the reset table next to ours. Linda had already opened the red one we'd been given. My stomach spun when she broke the seal and I heard the suck-hush of air.

When I tongued the roof of my mouth, I could taste last night. Yes, it did happen, and no, I didn't throw up. With a gap so big—this quarry inside me—how could one jam jar fill it?

Special

WE WATCHED THE SUNSET smear red over the glistening quarry. It was the end of our second summer without her. Loops of swallows. Arcs of fish. Quiet drips of sound, the day's wind tucked away. I recalled the story of the drowned woman. How she'd tied a rope to a rock to make that deadly anchor. That urge to disappear. I wondered if Cindy would understand that story now that she was older. Was my cousin tall and thin? Did she have short hair or long? I knew not to mention her name or ask about Aunt Doris.

I was doing what Dad had set me up to do again this summer — be a salesman like him. Dad sold envelopes. Big accounts with big companies like General Electric, Gerber and Canadian Tire while I sold bus tours in Niagara Falls. I was making good money working for Louie. No paycheques required, everything under the table. I didn't think about it being illegal. My success at selling was making Dad smile again.

Just the two of us, together, watching the sunset at the end of the day.

Dad was a man who could talk to anyone, anywhere. He had charisma. I didn't have charisma. How did I talk to strangers then, day after day? Fake sincerity, that's how. Separating truth from spiel. I didn't tell the tourists that ticket prices were negotiable or that they had to pay extra for admissions to the main attractions: Spanish Aero Car, Skylon Tower, the trip down the Niagara Gorge. I didn't tell them that the bus, an old green-painted school bus, wasn't air-conditioned or that the bus driver, a French Canadian with big biceps (he was always flexing them) drove at such a clipped pace, you barely had time to step out and say, "Cheese!" They trusted my girl-next-door ways.

Every week I made more money. The wads thick in their elastic bands. What other twenty-year-old brought cash to the bank in this small town? I felt my cheeks flush when I handed the money over to the teller. I didn't like bringing attention to myself the way Dad did. And yet, sometimes I felt a deep need for attention, for people to see me. It was an unsettling feeling.

I once considered keeping the money and spending it on extravagant clothes and flashy jewelry. I could pretend I was a character on *Dynasty* or *Dallas,* TV shows Mom loved to watch. But that thought didn't last. Besides, where would I go all dressed up?

"See, Dad?" I always said, flicking the proof. Canadian bills plus the bonus of American. "I beat yesterday's target."

"That a girl!" Dad said, his tanned face shining proudly.

He saw Linda while I was at work. She was off from teaching for the summer, and where she lived, about forty minutes away, meant she couldn't easily drop by. During those rare occasions when the three of us were together, his job of selling envelopes never came up. The other night when I asked him about it – he was slapping gobs of mayo onto his late-night sandwich – he said, "Like to keep my work life private. Got that?"

But dock time was our time. Our shared loss was with us then in the unbroken silence, the sun-setting glow over water, the red-driven blue.

He sighed deeply.

"What is it, Dad?" Soon I would be leaving for university again, my last year, was that it?

Then he told me his news. Talk of a new boss was looming at the envelope company, a young boss, very young. "M.B.A., my ass. He won't know the business. You build a business from reading books?"

Why go to university, then? If Mom were alive, I'd say this. I'd pounce on his contradiction. But I liked the flow we were in now, these evening talks about "raking in money." No one my age made the kind of cash I did. When I deposited those wads into my savings account, the bank teller's eyes snapped open.

He drew on the yellow pad he'd brought down to the dock with him, a straight line, horizontal. "They start you here," he said, "at the bottom. That's where you start." He leaned back for me to see, to take in the line. I nodded. "And then this." He drew a slanted line above the first line, forming a ten-degree angle. He didn't lean back this time but drew another line. "And this." Twenty degrees. Thirty. He kept going.

"I get it, Dad," I said, squirming, wanting him to stop. What did these lines have to do with a new boss? Where was he going with this? I felt a tingling sensation riding up my back. I couldn't take my eyes off his growing spray of lines.

He put the pen down between us on the dock bench.

"And like a tilt beneath your feet, you don't even feel it," he said. "Until—"

"You slide." I watched the pen roll and clatter onto the dock.

"Desperate people do desperate things." He was looking at the quarry now, at the growing darkness, as if he hadn't noticed the pen's fall.

I didn't like the word "desperate" or the way he'd said that expression. Was he talking about himself? I picked up the pen and tried to ignore the confusion I was feeling.

Dad rubbed the gentle roll of his hairy stomach. He checked his watch. "You don't need a swim tonight, do you? I'm starving. We've got cold cuts in the fridge and Linda's leftover potato salad."

I nodded like Mom used to, to show she was listening. I told myself I didn't need a swim. He wouldn't stop staring at me.

"You look so much like her."

THE DAY BEFORE leaving for university, I was sitting on the dock when Dad joined me. He was holding a jewelry box.

"Here," he said, removing the blue lid. "I want you to have it."

I lifted the silver ID bracelet from the cotton batting and tried to clasp it around my wrist.

"Gimme that," he said. His long fingers fumbled with the clasp, but he knew what to do. "There," he said, letting go.

I held my arm horizontally to read the cursive letters engraved on the silver plate, though I knew the words already: *Rusty, always my champion.*

He watched as I tested the fit.

"Beautiful, Russ," he said.

This time it didn't fall off.

ONE OF THE PRETTY GIRLS in residence who took over the common room daily asked me about the bracelet around my wrist. The purple chesterfields and cushions provided a canvas for her and the other long-haired blonde and brunette beauties, their thin bodies like lithe rivers. *The Young and the Restless.* A show I pretended to like. Another silly soap opera with drawn-out silences and phony dramatic monologues. But sometimes a storyline caught my attention and drew me in—the need to uncover the next family secret.

They called me "Bambi." They said I had a deer face. "Her eyes look like they're stuck in headlights." They said this as if I weren't there. But deer don't have blue eyes.

"She should see *Bambi Meets Godzilla,*" they said and giggled.

I pretended I'd seen the movie. In the original *Bambi,* the mother dies. Maybe that was the connection. They knew I'd lost a mother. Gossip about Mom's death had quickly circulated though my floor, the residence penthouse, when it happened. And I'd overheard enough comments to know what they thought of my post-Christmas return. "Imagine coming back so soon," they said. "If my mother died, I couldn't."

But that was months ago. No. More than a year ago. It was hard keeping track of time.

Now the bracelet ignited gossip.

"*Always my champion.* Oh!" they squealed in unison when I walked into the common room. I'd only told one of the girls where it came from. I hadn't thought through her over-friendliness.

So I stopped wearing it. At least during the week. I laid it out between the cotton strips and closed the blue box.

I should've known not to wear the bracelet in front of them. I thought back to last year's Valentine's Day. The residence rooms had hummed with excitement February 14th, with the constant buzzing of the intercoms, the messages from the residence ladies. *Delivery for you!* The giggles and squeals as the recipient raced down the hallway toward the elevators, then down the eleven floors, returning minutes later with a long white box in her slender arms.

I was stunned when the ladies buzzed my room. My mind rolled through possible suitors. Darren had been so long ago, and I hardly knew any boys at university. Perhaps that cute guy who sat near me in Statistics?

The florist's card in the mini white envelope provided the answer.

I tore it up. I didn't want anyone to see it. But it didn't matter, they knew.

WEEKENDS I WENT BACK to the quarry. We had our routines. Friday night: pizza or Chinese food. Saturday night: dinner at Chef's, the Italian restaurant across the border in the part of Buffalo where massive potholes punctured tires and thieves broke into parked cars. Chef's was famous for its secret sauce. The recipe never written down, the ingredients kept locked inside the chef's head. Local celebrities went there like Irv Weinstein, the pockmarked newscaster on *Eyewitness News*. The last time we saw him stuffing his face with their signature dish, parmesan pasta, Mom was with us. Only Mom could stop Dad from trying to get his attention.

There was always a wait. And they didn't take reservations. The mingling scents of garlic and tomato made your mouth water, so what a relief when the hostess finally called out your surname and you waded through the maze of tables with red-checkered tablecloths. Patrons always stared at Dad. His six-foot-six height commanded attention. So did his QT tan, the George Hamilton look, and his sharp casual clothes.

One night Linda did come with us. While she talked about her job, Dad the talker went quiet. Teachers were under attack for threatening to strike.

"They have no idea how demanding the job is," she said. "All they see is summers off." She looked at Dad. "There was talk of a CBC strike. Anything come of that?"

A forced politeness oozed from his barely-there smile. It made me feel strange. I could see it on Linda's face too, as clear as the clothes she was wearing – purple skirt and black silk blouse. She was thinking what I was thinking: *he's acting strange.*

"Linda, tell Caitlin what you're studying at school," Dad said, changing the subject. "That class of yours, that night class."

"Sure, Don."

She told me about her recent paper on behaviour modification, and we began to talk about Pavlov and his dogs. Ringing bells and salivation. For a brief moment, I forgot

Dad was there. Linda and I were immersed in a conversation as if we'd just met and were becoming friends. I wasn't thinking about how many calories I'd eaten or Dad's awkwardness. Dad knew nothing about Pavlov. "Sounds like a dessert," he said and laughed. "Which reminds me, did I tell you about the time..."

And the conversation turned to him.

THE FOLLOWING SATURDAY, Dad wanted me to go grocery shopping with him. I usually did when I came back to the quarry. He liked the company. But I didn't feel like going, so I told him I had to study. He never questioned that excuse.

The sun called through my bedroom window. I had to get out.

I walked around the quarry's edges and remembered how the three of us used to go out walking and exploring when we first moved here. Up and down the long gravel driveway, but also into the woods. Acres and acres of land surrounded the water-filled limestone pit, dense and lush and wooded land that edged the railway line, Windmill Point Road, Thunder Bay Road and Stonemill Road to form a grid that hid the blue oval from cars and trains and outside eyes. "You live by a quarry? Where?" people said to Mom and Dad, including locals. Our abode was a big blue secret.

During one of those walks, we came across an old stone fireplace in a grove of trees. The quarrymen must have cooked their meals there. Another time we found a glass bottle heap, a cairn of bottles from the turn of the century, most broken but some intact. Blue bottles for milk of magnesia, green for tonics, clear for milk – all caked in dirt. We gathered the good ones and brought them back to the house.

Mom washed them with a bottle brush to get the dirt out. She set them on the windowsill in the living room between her African violets. They streamlined the incoming light like the stained-glass windows in the United Church.

Things rustled behind the trees and inside the bushes. Rabbit, snake, bird and fox plus the odd escapee from the mink farm across Windmill Point Road. I'd never seen one alive before, only in books – weasel-long body and rodent face. But I knew their soft touch from Nana's church coat.

I would never wear a fur coat.

Today the light shimmered on the quarry water like a flattened disco ball. I wasn't wearing a jacket, but the sun warmed the cool breeze. Leaves were beginning to redden at the tips, but the scent of summer green was still present. Knee-high grasses shifted in the wind. They made the sound of river water as I made my way around the limestone edges into the goldenrod field that bridged the quarry from the middle of the driveway. When the river-sound stopped, that's when I saw her. Big eyes looked back at me from a tree-still body. Triangular face. Felt nose. Long legs, lean for leaping. Her coat glowed like her rusty tail, the white surrender turned down.

"Mom."

She twitched.

I moved closer.

But the sound of gravel came. The distant driveway flashed metallic blue. Dad's Caddy heading home.

When I turned, she was gone.

But the moment branded me.

After I told him about the deer, he closed the fridge and smiled and said, "I have something to tell you, too."

We sat down in his office. He, in his desk chair. Me, on the pullout couch.

"I woke to this light last night," he said, looking my way but not at me. "It came from down the hall, the living room. Faint at first. Then stronger, a full-on beam. I wanted to go to it, but my legs froze. The weirdest thing, I didn't panic. It got brighter and brighter – this feeling rushed in. 'Russ,' I said. 'That you?' The light glowed. When I tried to get up again, I could. But when I looked through the doorway, she was gone." He was looking at me now. "Well?" he said.

I was imagining the light, the rusty glow across the peg-wood floor, pure and warm and soundless. "I believe you, Dad."

We turned to the picture on the study wall above Mom's cedar chest. *Fire & Ice*. Mom's gift for Dad our first Christmas at the quarry. She hoped it would lessen the pain of his sister's deliberate absence.

As I stared at the image, a woman's silhouette emerged through the flaming curves of red, upwards from the block of ice.

"You see her, don't you," he said, staring at the picture.

"Yes, Dad. I see her."

Mom was no longer here to smooth any tension that spiralled between us, but her loss had become a catalyst. We needed her death to dispel our fights and disagreements. Just like Dad and I both needed our bad moods to help us witness her dying. We never talked about the slow deterioration that turned from monthly to weekly to daily to hourly until her breathing stopped. The cancer inside her kept coming back. She never complained. Not like Dad and I did. Dad mad at Nana – *She's rearranged the cutlery again, goddamn it.* Dad mad at me – *Why doesn't she get off the couch and do the dishes?* Me mad at Dad — *He's always telling me what to do, Mom. I'm sick of it.*

"You're my girl now," Dad said.

MY ROOMMATE SUZIE didn't like the pretty girls on our floor either. "Bitches," she called them. "Chick sticks." Her playful bitterness made me laugh. The kind of laughing I'd once had with my cousin Cindy, so long ago. Suzie liked having an audience. She liked to see me laughing. Yet we never became good friends. We didn't hang out together; we had separate lives outside Brandon Hall — her volleyball, my studies. I knew how to be on my own, the quarry had taught me.

I was shy about dressing and undressing in front of her, self-conscious of my body, my fleshy stomach and wobbly thighs. Suzie wasn't shy about her body. She walked around the dorm room in her bra and panties while brushing her scraggly hair. The action always ignited any static electricity in the room, making her brown strands fly.

One morning while Suzie was brushing out her blow-dried hair, she raised her arm high and I saw the dark mound. I couldn't help but stare at it. *So that's what happens when you stop shaving, an underarm beard.* I thought back to health class and the gym teacher's talk of body smells and fresh feminine hygiene. How a woman must take care of herself by practising good grooming.

I thought about my first time shaving. I was sitting at the edge of the dock, and Mom was smoking behind me. I soaked my legs with quarry water and lathered my calves with Ivory soap just like Mom had told me to do. Then I slid the razor through it, made pink paths. No nicks. The skin as smooth as the limestone water.

"Let's see, honey."

I held up my leg and set it on her lap.

"Yes," she said, touching it, not bothered by the soapy water dripping down her bare legs. "You've gone deep enough."

OUR DORM WINDOW faced the quad, Cootes Paradise sloped behind us, a nature trail that led to parts of the Royal Botanical Gardens, where ducks nested and other wildlife lived. I'd heard stories of girls getting attacked on those trails. What newspapers called "sexual assault." What victims knew as "rape." We'd discussed "sexual assault" in health class back in high school. The boys in a separate classroom so we'd be more comfortable "discussing our feelings." But who could be comfortable after watching that film? When I got home from school I told Mom about it.

"It's not always a stranger," she said. "It could be someone you know."

"You mean like a boyfriend?" I said. "Or a husband?"

She nodded. The end of her cigarette grew long and ashy.

"Do you know anyone that's happened to?"

She lit another cigarette, took a long drag and then blew the smoke out.

I waited.

"Who, Mom? Do I know her?" She turned to the window. A female cardinal landed beneath the feeder, in the scattered seeds. "Was it you, Mom?"

She wouldn't answer me.

Walking alone on those trails wasn't worth the risk. I had the quarry for walking, my own private sanctuary.

I was sick of studying for my cognition test. Suzie had just returned from showering after volleyball practice. The

McMaster Marauders were on a winning streak, which made me think of Mom and the trophies that filled the knick-knack shelves at the quarry. Dad kept them there like he kept all her things, even her clothes.

I started talking about the quarry—the fossils, the swimming, the nibbling-at-your-toes sunfish, the manic splashes carp made each spring when they rose to the surface to spawn.

"So, it's a lake," said Suzie.

"Well, a mini-lake. Forty feet deep in some spots."

"I prefer pools."

"They sting your eyes. The quarry doesn't."

"But those fish! Creepy."

Had I not described the quarry right? How could she think it was creepy? I turned to the window beside my bed. I liked looking outside our dorm room. People below had no idea you were watching them. The penthouse floor had its advantages—a bird's-eye view and no footsteps thumping above your head.

Across from Brandon Hall (the all-female residence) stood Woodstock (the all-male residence). You could see the long staircase through the large corner windows. Boys rarely took the stairs. I did. Climbing eleven flights helped burn extra calories. But today when I looked across, inside the top stairwell I saw arms waving, the arms of two boys.

I pulled back from the window. Were they waving at me? I hid behind the curtain and peeked out. They had stopped waving. When I returned to the window, they started again.

"Oh my God," I said.

"What. What is it?" Suzie raced to the window. I had to move to let her in. "A jumper?" she said, looking down before she followed my eyes. "Oh," she said. "Cool." She waved back.

"What are you doing?"

"What does it look like I'm doing?" She lifted my limp arm. "Come on, wave!"

"No," I said, putting my arm down.

"They're cute."

"You can't tell they're cute. You can barely see them."

"They're pointing down. See?" Suzie pointed down too. "Yes," she said. "They want to meet us."

"No."

"Why not? You look fine." She was fully dressed now, jeans and a tight white T-shirt. She smeared on her pearly fuchsia lipstick. "Here," she said, throwing me the tube. "And grab your jacket. Come on, it's about time you had some fun."

They were already standing in the quad when we walked out of Brandon Hall. Strands of white toilet paper, evidence of another wild night, were laced through the trees. They fluttered in the branches above the boys' heads. They said their names: Michael and Ernie.

I could tell Suzie liked Michael from the tilt of her neck, the way she thrust it forward like an offering, but Michael kept looking at me.

"I've seen you before," he said.

I smiled. He had a kind face. Round with round eyes that carried tints of yellow-green like grasses from the goldenrod field. He was taller than me, tall enough for me to set my chin on his shoulder. In my mind, we were already pressing bodies, clothed bodies, not naked. He looked familiar, too. Turns out we were in the same first-year chemistry class, in a lecture hall sized for three hundred.

"I knew I'd seen you before," he said after we'd figured it out.

"I was in that class," said Suzie. "Don't I look familiar?"

When Michael nudged Ernie, Ernie's face flushed pink, pink as the pimples lining his forehead and the hollow curves of his cheeks.

"I've seen you," said Ernie. He stared at Suzie. His eyes, dark buttons.

"In that chemistry class, right?" Suzie turned and tilted her neck toward him.

"No. In Woodstock."

Suzie looked away.

"You girls want to go for a walk?" asked Michael.

"Sure," said Suzie, moving beside him.

We headed around Brandon Hall and dipped under the canopy of branches that led to the trails. Michael cut across Suzie to walk beside me. My body tingled as I breathed in the leafy autumn smells. They mixed with the clean, soapy scent of Michael.

Suzie and Ernie continued to walk behind us. They were already a world away.

AFTER CLASSES THE NEXT DAY I arrived back at residence. One of the ladies behind the front desk called me over.

"Caitlin, there's a message for you."

Dad? No, Dad would phone. He wouldn't leave a message. A message meant a note from someone who'd dropped by to see you. Papers folded and tucked in alphabetized cubbyholes.

The ladies watched me read the note.

Caitlin M,

I don't know your favourite colour but hope these will do. Would love to see you again.

Michael

"Well, well," said the taller desk lady. They were both grey-haired. Their skin was pale and pasty. Ripe for Dad's QT.

The shorter one handed me a long white box.

Three of the pretty girls from my floor walked through the entrance. They huddled around me. "More flowers from Daddy-O?"

I stayed quiet. I couldn't think to talk.

In my room I reread Michael's note. There was a phone number at the bottom. After arranging the yellow roses in a glass vase, I called him.

"Thank you," I said. "They're beautiful."

"I hope you like yellow."

"I do," I said. Maybe I would now.

"Great," he said. "You don't seem like a red girl." He paused and cleared his throat. "You doing anything later tonight?"

"Just homework."

"Thought maybe we could go for a drink. You like to drink?"

I giggled. "Do you like to drink?"

"Stupid question. Sorry. Guess I'm nervous."

"It's okay," I said, staring at the roses on the shelf above my desk. I breathed in their fresh garden smell. "I really like them."

"Did they give you that powder stuff to make them last?"

"They did," I said. It had turned the tap water milky.

"I'm glad," he said. "I'm glad you like them. I've never sent flowers before. Have you ever gotten flowers?"

He wanted to be my first.

"You," I said.

"Cool," said Michael.

I smiled. From the lilt in his voice, I could tell he too was smiling.

MICHAEL SAID he didn't know what it was like to be an only child, since he had an older brother. But with a twelve-year difference between them, he said he knew what it was like to be alone.

"He's pretty much a stranger to me," said Michael. "He hardly ever comes home. He lives in Vancouver now."

But Michael still had his parents, and he was close to his mother. "You remind me of her," he said, taking hold of my hand. We were walking around the campus after studying in Mills Library. Michael, with his engineering books. Me, my psychology.

"I do? How?"

"It's hard to put into words. It's more like a feeling. Shit," he said. "I sound like an idiot."

"No, you don't." I squeezed his hand. "It's okay to have feelings and not understand them. That happens to me, too."

"Your mom, you mean. I'm sorry, Caitlin. That must be hard."

I nodded. Only then did I remember last night. "You okay, Caitlin?" Suzie had whispered after I jolted out of my nightmare. I must've been crying out in my sleep.

If Michael thought I was like his mother, was his mother like mine? I felt the sudden urge to meet her.

"Have you ever lost anybody you loved?" We were walking through the stone archway of Hamilton Hall, the oldest building on campus, when I asked that. The walls were riddled with ivy. The green leaves had turned red and were now fading to grey from the falling dusk.

"No, not like that. Listen," he said. "Let's see a movie this weekend. My treat."

"I'd love to —"

"Great," he said.

Through the creamy gleam of the streetlight, I saw his radiant smile. I wanted to keep that smile there, but given my father and his weekend demands, I knew I had my work cut out for me.

I CHEWED MY PEN and crossed and uncrossed my legs under my desk. I couldn't concentrate on the chart I was making for my Behaviour Modification class. Red light pecks. Green light pecks. Pellets given. Pellets withheld. Bird course. The term we used for a class that was a piece of cake. But this bird course had a bird, a pigeon I'd christened Red. We'd all been assigned our own pigeons. We kept them in individual cages in the basement of the Psych Building. Seventy-five percent of its body weight, the magic number to maintain — hungry enough to peck at a light but not hungry enough to not peck.

"The only way to fail this course," said Dr. Hudson, the bald-headed pigeon assigner, "is to end up with a dead bird." He smiled as we laughed. "No casualties, please!"

Red had done what she was supposed to do in her Skinner box — perform three clockwise turns before pecking at a green light and one counter-clockwise turn before pecking at a red light. Her little superstitious dance had begun by chance, but now she re-enacted it to bring forth the reward, the food pellet. She had no idea I'd shaped her behaviour. For the chart, I was tallying up the number of pellets it had taken Red to reach that place of magical thinking: I do this, I get that. I kept staring at the phone.

As far as Dad knew, I was coming home this weekend. As far as Michael knew, I was spending it with him. And now I had to pee again.

After entering the end cubicle, I heard the washroom door whoosh open.

"I knew something was up. Slut. Just because she's on the volleyball team."

"Room Service," said the other voice. "They call her that too, Beast and the boys. I hear she's working her way down the floors now."

"Think Caitlin knows?"

"She's too wrapped up with Daddy-O."

"I hear she's got a guy."

"No way. Really?"

"From Woodstock."

"Well, I wonder if Suzie's sucked him off too. I could ask Beast."

Rinse and spit and *whoosh*, they were gone.

I put my feet down.

So, my roommate was a sex maniac.

I'd heard of "Beast," the rumoured leader of the rumoured Pigfest, the underground frosh week competition which guys were challenged to bring the ugliest girl on campus to their dorm room. The guy with the ugliest – *the pig* – won. I thought back to the day we'd met Michael and Ernie in the quad, how Ernie had seen Suzie in Woodstock. Had something happened? Had she been too drunk to remember?

Michael hadn't taken part in Pigfest. I felt this knowing in my bones. The same way my body had felt a knowing for other things. Like the way it knew Mom had cancer before they told me she had cancer. Like the way it knew she'd die on Christmas Day. This knowing rippled inside me and said: *you can trust Michael.*

"GOT YOUR FAVOURITE ICE CREAM, that hash stuff you like," Dad said on the phone. "We'll order Chinese Friday, see a matinee Saturday."

My stomach prickled the way it had a moment ago when I dialled my home number. "I thought I'd stay here this weekend, Dad."

The sound of drumming fingers on wood, an intake of breath.

"Dad?"

"What do you mean? You're joking, right? You can study here. I'll let you study."

"It's not about studying."

A deeper intake of breath.

"Oh, I see. A boy, is it?" The drumming continued. No doubt his knee was jackhammering under his desk. Finally, he spoke. "When am I going to meet him?"

"What about *our* plans?" Michael said, later that night. "*St. Elmo's Fire?*"

"I know," I said and slowed to his step. A gust of dry yellow leaves flew across the campus path. Michael kicked his way through them. "I'm sorry, Michael. Can we see it next week?"

He led me to the nearest bench, the one closest to Brandon Hall.

"Let me give you a ride, then," he said, sitting beside me. "I could meet your dad. See the quarry."

The next day Michael came by for me in a pickup truck that once belonged to his father, and we headed down the QEW.

"I want to hear what your dad's like," I said.

"He likes to talk. He's always talking, always turning the conversation toward himself. Me, me, me." Michael hit the steering wheel to the beat of each "me" as if drumming a pop song. The truck's interior reeked of cigar smoke even with the windows half-open. I was glad Michael didn't smoke cigars like his father. "Once he made me so mad, I went to my room and put a sticker on the bottom of my door. The kind you find in a cereal box for assembling a game or something. A lightning bolt."

"And?"

"That's it. That's what I did. So I'd remember how mad he made me. How about your dad? What's he like?"

"He's a talker. He commands the room."

"He sounds intense. What's he do—"

"Michael. Look at those trees."

The Niagara Escarpment was clothed in fall colours. They made me think of our kitchen carpet back at the quarry. It was then that I realized we were driving through a massive quarry, a pit carved by a glacier's hands. No dynamite required here to cut stone. No underground springs to seep back up, just fertile earth for growing peaches and cherries and grapes. Fruitbelt. We passed the exit for Grimsby.

Hard to believe I ever lived there. Maybe Michael was right to mark his anger with a sticker. A mark that signalled: *I feel*. But only Michael would know the meaning behind it. Otherwise, it was a mute lightning bolt with no story to tell.

"What did he do, Michael?"

"Sold life insurance. Still does."

"No, I mean what did he do to make you so angry?"

We were past the fields of fruit trees now. I turned down the radio before repeating my question.

"What did he do?"

"It's okay, Caitlin. I heard you the first time." He gripped the wheel with both hands.

"Not to worry," I said lightly. "It doesn't matter." Perhaps it was better I didn't know. I was about to turn the radio back up when Michael nudged me from touching the volume button.

"I don't remember, okay?" he said. "But that's not the point. The point is I needed to remember the feeling."

I thought of the jar of red jam I'd kept from our trip to New York City. It was tucked in the back of my dorm-room dresser.

"Oh," I said, nodding.

The wind came through like a voice gone quiet. It travelled the interior and wrapped us as one.

"You sure you're okay with this? Driving me there and then driving back. It's a long drive."

Michael checked the clock on the dashboard. "We're making good time. No traffic. Drive back'll be quicker."

"Yes," I said, knowing he'd slowed down for me. I didn't mind passing transport trucks, but I wasn't one for speed.

"Wow," he said. "Look at that."

The sun hovered over a low-lying cornfield, a big fist of blood. "I wish you could've met her," I said, my eyes fixed on the red.

"I know. But I am meeting her, right? She's part of you." He put his hand on my thigh and left it there. The steady hush of tires over tarmac.

"She never complained. All that pain. Her body decaying. Cells spreading. Cells you can't stop —"

"My mother keeps things in too. She's like that."

"Your mother doesn't have cancer. She's not *like that*."

"Caitlin?"

"You have a mother."

He lifted his hand from my thigh. "I've upset you. I'm sorry."

"No," I said, putting his hand back. "It's me who's sorry."

When Michael steered the truck around the bend of our long gravel driveway, he got his first view of the quarry. "Wow. It's a lake. You really are in the middle of nowhere." He stopped on impulse and we stepped out of the truck. "You swam across that?" he said, taking hold of my hand.

"Around it, too."

"Looks cold," he said as we walked toward it. Waves but no whitecaps. I could see Dad's Eldorado parked in the carport beside Mom's Malibu, but the line of tall cottonwoods would prevent him from seeing us. When I looked to the sky, I saw movement.

"The osprey," I said. "He's back."

The bird of prey circled the quarry and stilled. Down he came, feet first. He hit the water hard with a forceful splash, and his body went under until he flapped back up through the white-water spray. The fish twisted in his grip, the beak-like talons, but the osprey held on.

"Jesus, you don't see that every day," Michael said, stepping over a grapevine to get a closer look. "I think he's got a smallmouth."

We got back into the truck and Michael parked under the carport, in Nana's old space, then we walked down the path to the side door. Words of introduction swam through my head: Dad, this is my boyfriend, Michael. *No, not right.*

Dad, I'd like you to meet a special friend of mine. *No, not right either*. I was still debating what to say when I turned the knob of the unlocked door and we strode in.

There in the middle of the kitchen stood my startled father in baggy blue boxers and white gym socks.

"Oh, goddamn," he said and put down his beer.

Michael put out his hand like it was the thing to do, the only thing when confronted with one's girlfriend's father, red-faced, half-naked.

"Hello, Don," said Michael, shaking my father's hand.

He cringed at the sound of his first name. "I'm getting changed," he said, letting go of the handshake. He turned to the doorway that led toward the master bedroom.

I led Michael through the other doorway, into the family room. I didn't want him to see the butt of Dad's underwear; God knows there might be skid marks. We looked out the window, at what we could see, given daylight was leaving. We eyed each other and smiled but didn't break into laughter. We knew Dad would hear us. He'd turned the radio off.

"Sit," Dad said when he came back in. He was tying the string of his cotton track pants.

"I'll stand," Michael said, rubbing his back. "Long trip."

I sat.

But Dad didn't sit. He wasn't about to look up at the new man in my life, a man who dared to call him "Don," not "Mr. Maharg." He remained standing.

"I hear you're an engineer."

"Will be in a couple of years, if all goes well." Michael wriggled his right pinkie finger. "I'll have an iron ring."

"You know how to work with your hands?" He looked at Michael's hands as if they had the answer.

"Yeah, I know how to work with my hands."

"Good," Dad said, cocking his head. "You can help me trim that bugger of a hedge."

"Dad," I said. "It's getting dark out. Michael has to drive back to Hamilton."

Dad looked out the window. "Plenty of light out there."

I looked at Michael, who was looking at my father. Their eyes like wrestling hands.

"Plenty of light," said Michael, eyeing the hedge.

Moments later I shouted over the loud chirr of the electric hedge trimmer. "If this isn't dark, I don't know what is!" They were taking turns holding the ladder, climbing up the rungs, climbing back down. They were in their own battle now. The prize – me – pointless. It got maddening standing there in the cold dark, so I went back inside and took the heavenly hash out of the freezer. Setting the container on top of the tea towel I'd spread over my lap, I spooned cold, numbing mounds into my mouth.

Something inside me said *stop*. I fastened the lid before the spoon touched bottom. The rim's *click* gave a pleasing sound like the snap of a hole closing in. I wanted my insides to do that – snap to a shut my ears could hear. But the shutting inside me was faint like an echo.

I was cradling the container when I realized what I was touching. Condensation made the *Special* sticker easy to remove. It lifted off in one piece. The orange shone brightly on my index finger, and the black letters popped.

I shoved the ice cream back in the freezer and walked down the hall to my bedroom. My finger glowed like an orange sucker. I knelt beside my bedroom door and stuck *Special* to the bottom of it.

Don't Swallow

EVERY OTHER SUNDAY, Mr. and Mrs. Vargo dropped by Brandon Hall to pick their daughter up and take her to church. Two hours later, Suzie came back to the dorm room with a food basket. Garlicky meats, toe-sized pickles, Sunkist oranges and always a special treat: Chips Ahoy! chocolate-chip cookies.

I hadn't confronted Suzie about her secret life as "Room Service" but she must've known that I knew. Weekends I wasn't there, she used our room as her base. Guys in. Guys out. The girls on our floor saw her sneaking them in.

I was too embarrassed to do anything about it, though she must've sensed the subtle changes between us, the lengthening silences and the declining laughter. Sometimes while she blow-dried her hair, I stared at her fuchsia lips.

I only took one cookie. Nibbled it like a mouse, alone in our room after dinner. I let the chocolate chips melt on my tongue and mix with the crumbs. I resealed the bag but couldn't get the folds right. *She'll know.* I reopened the bag and tried again, and the siren smell wafted back up. *One more won't make any difference.* By the time she returned from volleyball practice, I'd eaten the whole row.

The next evening, I ate another row. I did the same the night after that. Why bother hiding it? She knew what I was doing now. But like me she didn't say anything.

We kept hold of each other's secrets.

The sweet taste of cookies brought back the memory of Mom's cookie dough, her weekly call from upstairs – *Come lick the bowl!* – when we lived at the Upside-Down House. I'd drop my Barbies on the bedroom floor and race up the stairs into the turquoise kitchen, kneel on the kitchen chair she'd set by the counter, grab hold of the spatula and lick. While the dough balls baked in the oven, I fingered the insides of the ceramic bowl.

One night, bloated with disgust from eating more than one row of Suzie's cookies, I found a deserted washroom on another floor of Brandon Hall. Gathering my hair with one hand, I knelt down and faced the toilet, hooked my fingers down my raw throat and heaved the chew out of me.

"YOU'RE PERFECT," Michael said, eyeing my naked body, making me blush as I pulled the bedsheets over me.

We were lying on my residence bed. With Suzie away at a volleyball meet, we had the room to ourselves.

We knew how to touch each other, the finger rhythms

we needed. We didn't take long. Michael crumpled his moist Kleenex.

But my grieving body couldn't handle him inside me, too much pain.

"What's wrong, Caitlin?" Michael had said our first time. We were on the same bed we were on now.

"I don't know," I said, trying to understand it. What I wanted with my mind wasn't there in my body. The hole for us closed to him.

"Grief takes time." He rubbed my arm, a gesture meant to soothe, but it made me flinch. His voice had taken on the annoying tone of the new book he was reading: *How to Help a Loved One Through Grief.*

"You don't know," I said, sitting up, pressing the bleached sheet to my stomach, trying to make sense of the piercing, the lingering sting. He'd want to go inside me again. A fork jamming for an oyster.

But Michael was patient. He began a series of romantic gestures. Massage oil one night. Soft music the next. Expensive French wine. "Relax," he said the night he tried all three. "I'll take care of you." He kissed my neck the way Darren used to, though it didn't make me tingle the same way. When Michael massaged my shoulders, I felt them loosen, but the hidden core held tight, that final give he wanted to take.

"Why?" I said. I could feel my eyes brimming. Did this happen to Mom, too? "I don't understand," I said and turned to hide the rising tears. And then I saw, in the shadow of shifting candlelight, a glitter of pink through the slit of Suzie's closet.

"Wait," I said and got up to cross the room. I yanked Suzie's tube top off the wire hanger and slipped it on.

He sat up to watch.

I slipped out of my underwear and kept the pink glitter on, knelt on the floor beside him while he lay on my bed. "You're tense," I said. "Let me take care of you." I took him into the cavity of my mouth, licked the veins, the blue tributaries, the skin stretched like the skin of a drum. He made a sloppy rolling sound between rising moans. He was almost ready. Salt on my tongue from the secretion on his tip.

Nervosa

HE PACED THE LENGTH of the blackboard as he talked and pressed his hands behind his back to think – his catch-phrase, *basic emotions*. Who knew individuals liked to eat dirt? Pull hair out by the roots? Cut their skin? And the names of disorders I didn't want to acknowledge: anorexia nervosa, bulimia nervosa. That's not me. I haven't eaten from the Chips Ahoy! bag for three days. *But you're thinking about them, aren't you? The impulse, the silent urges, weighing yourself every weekend – feeling defeated when the needle won't go down.*

"Caitlin, may I speak with you for a moment?"

He was watching me descend the lecture hall steps. He stood at the bottom waiting. When my sneakers touched floor level, I had to look up. A grey patch lined the trim curve of his dark brown beard. I felt the urge to touch it. The sheen on his forehead shone into a star.

"It's about your topic."

I followed him to the lectern. He pulled out my proposal. The red circles glistened.

"You've yoked the two eating disorders. I only need the one." He handed back the proposal. "You'll have to choose."

"Oh," I said. "I didn't realize." The red circles vibrated.

"I'll give you some time to think about it, but I'll need to know your choice soon. Drop by my office. Third floor. Room 303." He snapped his briefcase shut. "Come, I'll walk you out."

"Dr. Delio?" said a creamy voice. The female student was standing in the hallway, leaning on the opposite wall. You could tell from her pose she'd been waiting. "Can I talk to you for a minute?" Thin and pretty, a perky reminder of all I'd never be. "Or I could meet you in your office later."

"That won't be necessary. We can talk now." He turned to me and smiled. "See you soon, Caitlin."

It had neurological, psychological and sociological components. The adjectival form meant a lack of desire to eat, but the eating disorder needed both words to cover its range. Take away the first word – *anorexia* – and all you had was *nervosa,* a reduced appetite.

Those last days in the hospital, Mom couldn't use her mouth. An IV tube did the trick. Her needled hand, a splay of bone beneath my fleshy fingers.

The second disorder on my proposal was a *nervosa* too. The first word of the two-word term derived from "a ravenous hunger." You eat and eat until you can't eat anymore, and then you throw up.

She had come back to me as a deer, to Dad as moving light. Comforting visits. But she'd also come back as a horror show. Pus and scab through a white wedding dress, a hand in an open coffin, ready to grab me.

When I arrived at Dr. Delio's office door two days later, he invited me in and told me to sit down.

"So, how are you?" he said. "Enjoying the class?"

"Yes," I said. "It's a good class."

"No complaints then?"

"No complaints."

After looking at my proposal for a moment, he set it down on his paper-strewn desk. "We'll get to this." He smiled.

I smiled back.

"There," he said. "That's what's missing."

"Missing?"

"Your smile. I knew you had one." He leaned back in his office chair. "You always look so sad."

"I do?" I could feel myself blushing.

"Roommate troubles? No. That's not it. Something more serious. Am I right?"

I nodded.

He tapped my paper. "Disorders like this don't just happen. There's always a link to some kind of catalyst. I'm thinking you know this."

"Loss," I said. "I lost my mother." My eyes welled up.

He rolled his chair forward. A musky, oily scent. Different from Michael's clean scent. It tunnelled my insides. He shook his head. "How long ago?"

"The Christmas before last. She died Christmas Day."

"Oh," he said. "That's hard. Cancer?"

"How did you know?"

"A gut feeling. I bet you have those too, gut feelings."

I nodded.

"I know what loss is," he said. "It takes a long time. You're not sleeping, are you?"

"I look tired?"

"A little."

And then I told him what had kept me up last night—Mom in an open coffin, trying to grab me. But I didn't tell him what I did afterwards, how I ate all the sticky contents of the last jar of St. Regis red jam, then shoved a finger down my throat.

He raised his arms over his head, entwined his fingers. "Is it a recurring dream?"

"It's horrible." I touched my face to cool the warmth there. "I can't believe I'm telling you this."

His shoulders loosened as he rolled his chair toward me. I could smell his earthy cologne again—or was it him, his scent?

"May I suggest talking to the image? Enter the dream and confront it. Say something like—*you're not my mother, she wouldn't do this to me.* Call the nightmare's bluff. Does this make sense?"

"I think so."

He picked up the paper. "Do the two disorders. No need to choose."

"Really? Thanks."

"Dr. Delio?" said a female voice. The blonde again? I turned to see who was at the door. No, another student. Not so pretty. Not so thin. "Is now a good time?" she said, eyeing me.

"Thank you," I said, and stood up. I grabbed hold of my knapsack.

"Okay, Janet, come in, come in. See you soon, Caitlin. Let me know what happens."

Janet squeezed by me – I was almost out the door when he said, "Caitlin?"

When I turned he was smiling. I could see his straight teeth. I couldn't help but smile back.

"Let me know soon."

As I walked down the empty hallway and into the ladies' room, a glow spread through me. It was there in my face when I looked in the mirror. A red glow. A glow that said: *alive*.

The next time the decaying body of my mother rose from the open coffin and the flesh-blackened hand attempted to grab, I didn't recoil with a silent scream. I pushed my voice into the nightmare. I talked to the dead.

I couldn't wait to tell him. "I did what you told me to do," I said when I arrived at his office the following Tuesday. "I talked back to it."

"Good! Excellent," said Dr. Delio. He pressed his hands together.

"It hasn't come back since," I said, shaking the snow from my hair, the first snowfall of the year.

"Closure," he said, grinning. "That's what you needed." He removed the stack of papers from the chair I'd sat on during my last visit. He patted the emptiness. "I want to hear all about it."

From that point on, Tuesday became our day.

THOSE FIRST FEW VISITS he closed the office door when I arrived. Now I did. I told him about Dad and Nana and the mother I missed. He wanted to know what it was like living with all that tension under one roof.

"She kept everything – elastic bands, bread ties. She'd slap me on the arm if she saw me throwing them out. They

163

sat on the kitchen windowsill, tons of them, doing nothing but piling up. And she was always moving things, from cupboard to cupboard, rearranging the cutlery drawers. Dad could never find a teaspoon to stir his coffee. He'd curse her name under his breath. She was always at him."

"And your mother?"

I thought of Nana's deliberate silence when Mom lived in the red brick house, pointed and punishing silence to make her daughter feel worthless, invisible.

"Mom has cancer," I said. "Nana has to be nice to her. Had, I mean."

"And you? What did she think of her granddaughter?"

The grey flecks of Dr. Delio's beard held the shade of Nana's hair, the long, grey coils she'd loop into two snakes, their hisses absorbed by hairpins. One night while I was trying to sleep, they unravelled in my mind into a mass of grey slithering snakes, squirming on her pillow as she slept.

"Me?" I straightened in the chair as if Nana were suddenly present. "I stayed out of her way. She was always watching."

I was about to say, "She threw out my stuffed Lambie," when he asked, "And your father, how's he doing now?"

"Okay, I guess. He's met someone. Linda. He acts weird when he's around her, at least when I'm around. They see each other during the week and on weekends when I'm here. He's always pressuring me to come home."

"Only child... He wants you all to himself then, does he?" Dr. Delio didn't wear a ring on his left hand, but I knew from student gossip that he was married, a father of two.

"You said you know loss... Your mother?"

He closed his eyes. "Father," he said, and took a deep breath. "He hung himself."

164

"No," I said. "How horrible." And then I knew. "You found him, didn't you?"

"It was hell, Caitlin," he said, opening his eyes. The wheels of his chair rolled forward, and the tip of his knee touched mine.

But it wasn't hell talking about it. This was the becoming of us.

HE LENT ME BOOKS and academic journals. Readings that went deeper than the sources on the term paper he'd graded me A+. Xerox copies of his published studies in respected journals. His full name in print: *Daniel Ray Delio, Ph.D. Associate Professor.*

One afternoon while I sat in his third-floor office, we talked about dreams. Mine were so vivid now. Were they always so vivid? Or did Mom's death make that happen? In my most recent dream, I was standing in the middle of a dark road, a car coming toward me, bright headlights, brighter, time to move, but I couldn't move, my feet were stuck, and when I looked down at my feet, they were elongated toes, and when I touched my head, I felt velvet-covered branches growing out of my skull – was it bone? – bushy feeling with a waxy coating, hot to the touch as if heated from within. When I went to the library, I found out this: *Antlers are made of true bone that is fed by blood which is carried in the outer velvet covering. Velvet antlers are hot to the touch, with brushy hair and a waxy coating.*

"The car drove through me." I shuddered. He saw me shudder. "And then I woke up."

"Vivid inner life," he said. "Not everyone has that."

I mentioned Michael then, his inability to remember his

dreams. "But he must dream, right? He says he doesn't, but I think it's because he doesn't remember."

"He dreams. You're right. But maybe too deeply for recall. Helen doesn't remember her dreams either."

I waited. I was eager for him to keep going. Helen Delio. Her name on his lips.

"Dreams…" he said. "It doesn't matter. She's not interested in what I do here. The twins keep her busy. This Michael, he your boyfriend?"

I dug my nails into my skin, little half-moons. I tried not to squirm. "We kinda see each other."

"Kinda see each other." He chuckled. "Is that what they're calling it now?" He eyed me closely.

"We – Michael and I – we don't talk like this."

He winked. "What we have is special then?"

Someone knocked on his office door, and his smile turned into a frown. "Here they come again, the needy ones." He flicked his pen across his desk and stood up. "Don't they see my office hours?" He leaned in closely and whispered, "I'm tempted to ignore her, but no doubt she's heard us."

He was right, it was a she. Another she I didn't know. But I left his office with the whisper of his warm breath in my ear.

I understood more about my mother now, thanks to Dr. Delio. Why she'd kept her cancer a secret, the maternal need to protect her only child. And when I told him how I'd spent so much time away from the house – at Brenda's or Hideaway Park, or swimming in the quarry – he said that it was my coping mechanism. I'd retreated physically *and* emotionally before my mother's death as a method of preparation. It was all subconscious. I didn't have to feel guilty about it. (Though I did.) I understood more about Nana, too.

"You lost a mother, Caitlin, but your grandmother lost a daughter." He helped me see other points of view. "I bet you look just like your mother," he'd said. "I don't know," I told him. "People tell me I do, even more now. I must be growing into her." These realizations comforted me as the spring term wound to an end, and the compulsion to devour Suzie's Chips Ahoy! cookies gradually disappeared.

He knew things about me that nobody else did. Not Dad. Not Michael.

"Any more thoughts on your independent study?" he said the last week of classes.

"I'm thinking about working with Dr. Hudson. I had fun working with my pigeon, Red." *What had happened to Red? Is she still doing that little dance? Is she alive?*

Dr. Delio crossed his arms.

"Kidding." I grinned. "Of course I want to work with you."

He stroked his beard. "Miss Caitlin Maharg, consider your application accepted."

I DIDN'T WANT TO go back to the quarry that summer. I wanted to work in Montreal. Suzie had gotten a summer job there at an English-speaking restaurant, and she said they were looking for more waitresses. We worked well as room-mates, and we'd save money sharing an apartment. "You should come," she said.

I didn't want to go back to the quarry, back to selling bus tours and listening to Dad talk about his latest troubles, the new boss he couldn't stand, the young boss with the M.B.A. He was thinking about leaving the company, the one he'd been with for close to thirty years. Abandoning the old ship and boarding that of the fresh competition: Innovation Envelopes.

Dad still took selling seriously. Each sales pitch was like a new performance, like opening night in the theatre or the key scene in a movie.

"Play the part as if you're playing for an Academy Award nomination," he'd said to Louie the summer I started selling bus tours.

Louie smiled and said, "Go stand behind one of my goddamn booths then." They were standing on the veranda, looking out at The Hill and they didn't know I was behind them on the other side of the screen door of the Niagara Clifton Motor Inn. "Bring me back some big bucks," said Louie, "and I'll give you an award."

Dad laughed. "She's doing good though, eh, Lou?"

Louie nodded.

"I told Russ she'd be all right."

The weekend before my last exam of my last year at university, it was warm enough to be on the dock, so Dad and I sat outside with our windbreakers caped around us. The nylon edges flapped with each burst of breeze. Dad sipped his Labatt's. He was staring at me.

"What?"

He looked so much older now. Grief. What QT couldn't hide. Deeply etched lines of missing Rusty on his forehead, the cutting lines around his mouth, the dark circles.

I prepared for a fight. I'd stand my ground.

"I want to work in Montreal this summer," I said in a rush. "Suzie's got a job there and they need other waitresses and it's a fancy restaurant and I'll make good tips."

"Oh. And where would you live?" he asked after a lengthy silence.

"Suzie's got an apartment there. A sublet."

"I see. It's all set then."

I tried to release the tension I'd bottled up by moving my legs back and forth. I had expected he'd be yelling at me by now. A fish jumped through the sun's red blade. "So, you're okay with this?"

He leaned forward and put both hands on his head. Was he crying?

"Dad? You okay?"

"I know you're not a little girl anymore. I know that. But you being here, for one more summer, would mean a lot to me. Everything's ahead of you." He looked out at the quarry before looking back at me.

His eyes were blue and viscous and lined with arterial wires. What I saw inside of them pulled at my insides, past the guilt that made me so angry, toward my deepest self.

"Okay. I'll stay."

"That's my girl," he said, leaning back, exhaling.

River of Hands

"YOU'RE STAYING INSIDE THE LINES," said Suzie when I told her I wasn't going to Montreal this summer. It was the end of exams, and we were packing up our belongings to vacate our dorm room. She dropped the pink glitter tube top into her suitcase.

"What's that supposed to mean?"

"He has you where he wants –"

"You think it's easy to say no to him? I'm all he has."

"He has Linda."

"She isn't flesh and blood to him."

"Well, neither was your mother."

I took a deep breath to ease the sting. Why did her comment bother me? I was the bloodline between my parents. Of course they weren't related.

"You're old enough to do what you want. But, hey, don't listen to me. What do I know? I'm just a slut."

"I never said that."

"Oh, come on. I know what they say about me. Think I care? Life is here to take, Caitlin, to colour *outside* the lines. I know you know that—you won't admit it."

"When did you get so wise?"

"Michael isn't enough for you—and yet you cling to him."

"I do not."

"What about your friendship with Dr. Delio?"

She was throwing so many thoughts at me that I had to sit down. I slid my open suitcase across the stripped mattress to make room. "I'm not you."

"You got that right."

I was about to respond when our room buzzer rang.

"Yes?" said Suzie into the intercom.

"Mr. Maharg is here."

She looked hard at me. "His daughter will be right down."

DAD WAS LEANING ON the front desk counter, making the residence ladies giggle like adolescent girls again. The lobby was busy with parents and daughters coming and going. I put down my suitcase in the middle of the lobby. It made a loud thump. With all the anger and confusion racing through me, I hadn't felt how heavy it was. All that time together in our penthouse dorm, and it ends like this. A cutting feeling radiated through me.

"There's my girl," said Dad, turning toward me. He was energized from charming the ladies, but he still looked tired. He was wearing his pink alligator T-shirt, the one Linda liked. He smiled. I didn't smile back. I walked through the open sliding glass doors, deliberately leaving my suitcase behind, and hopped into the passenger seat of the Caddy.

"Jesus, what you got in that?" Dad said, slamming the trunk. He got into the driver's seat and pulled the shoulder strap across his chest without clicking it in, the way he always did. "A dead body?"

I could tell he was smiling from the way he said that. My anger heightened.

"Where's your nice boyfriend? Why wasn't he carrying your suitcase for you?"

I refused to look at him and stared out the side window. Michael was writing his last exam. We had said our goodbyes yesterday. "Stay close to the phone tomorrow night," he'd said. I knew what that meant, who he didn't want to talk to. Dad grabbed for his Halls.

We were almost off campus now. I didn't want to leave McMaster. I wanted to be walking under the stone archway of Hamilton Hall, en route to the Psych Building's third floor. Dr. Delio would understand this. *Staying inside the lines.* How dare she say that.

"Louie's got you all set up at Canuck again. It'll be slow until the season kicks in, but you know that."

The radio was on low, but I could hear a high-octane voice from an annoying ad: *It's worth the drive to Acton!* When it finally ended, a song came on. I knew the song from a long time ago. I knew what it meant. Dad turned up the volume. "Hey, when's the last time you heard this one?" It took Dad longer to recognize the song, it always did. Not me. I knew a song's identity by the first few notes, even with low volume. My listening was always attuned. Mom had said it was a gift to recognize a song so quickly.

She'd witnessed it whenever we watched *Name That Tune* together.

"I can name that tune in...five notes," said the first contestant.

"Three notes," said the opponent.

"One note."

"Name that tune."

Some gift. What would I do with it?

I closed my eyes and listened. There I was in the front seat of the Malibu, the top down, the leather seat sticky beneath my bare legs, my fingers sticky from holding the chocolate ripple ice cream cone. Just Dad and I doing Saturday errands together. *Cruisin'* Dad called our special outings. *Let's go cruisin'.* The summer sun beating down on us – light and light and more light – not darkness and death. Mom at home sleeping after her ICU nightshift, a little girl happy to be sitting next to her bigger-than-life father.

"Come on! Sing, Caitlin. *Tie a yellow ribbon round the ole oak tree...*" He touched the Caddy's ceiling. "I'd put the top down if I could."

He continued singing in his over-the-top voice. He was enjoying this. *He has you where he wants you.* Suzie's words rattled through me.

I reached for the volume and turned it off. Then I blurted: "I'm-going-to-Montreal-next-summer. I won't be coming home."

He continued staring straight ahead, but his shoulders stiffened. The rhythmic sound of wheels on highway filled the silence. Then came a jiggling sound from the back seat, something metal shaking. It had happened before. Dad hated the sound. He'd make me hunt it down, but we could never find the source.

He squeezed my knee. "Come on, sing with me. This'll stop that damn noise for now." He turned the radio back on. The song was over.

I WAS SITTING ON THE DOCK, looking out at the quarry. Little ripples came and went with the soft breeze. This damn summer, weather permitting, my goal was to swim every day. Long swims, the evidence on my fingertips, wrinkled doughy flesh. I wanted to be thin when September came. We'd see each other often because of my independent study: "The Effects of Prenatal Stress on Litter Size in Mice." I'd originally hoped for his other research topic–suicide–but he'd put that on hold. Publish or perish. There was always that pressure. So what if I didn't get my first choice? I'd be near him more than ever my last year.

The earlier rainfall lingered on the dock. The towel I was sitting on helped my bottom stay dry. Dad was still sleeping. He and Louie had gone to Buffalo last night to watch a baseball game at a local bar. The Expos were on a roll. "Why can't you watch it at home?" I'd heard Linda ask Dad yesterday. She was cutting celery for the potato salad. Dad loved her potato salad, along with her macaroni salad. "Family recipes," said Linda. The contents sticky and goopy – saturated with mayonnaise. But I ate them both anyway, and I'd eaten too much last night, so I wanted to swim even more laps today. I wasn't supposed to swim alone. But if I had to be here all summer, why shouldn't I swim when I want? Besides, how would Dad save me if I were drowning?

He was mad at me last night. He told me to watch my tone before he drove off to meet Louie. Linda had already gone by then. She never stayed very long when I appeared.

He said I was being snippy. "Go jump in the lake!" he yelled.

"Okay!" I snapped back.

My lake, my quarry.

He'd been making snide comments about Michael again. Michael hated coming here. Just like Darren. But I knew if I asked Michael, he would come. He would do that for me. Though he refused to call Dad "Mr. Maharg." "We're adults, Caitlin. Come on. Don'll get over it." But Dad flinched whenever Michael called him by his first name. I could feel the tension. My skin would do that — absorb his pings of injury.

Part of me secretly hoped Dad's unwelcoming ways would become too big a barrier for Michael and he wouldn't visit much this summer. I could be alone with my thoughts and daydream about Dr. Delio. Michael's presence intensified my guilt. As if I'd swallowed sixty worry dolls and they were attacking my insides, poking me with their wiry feet. "You'll miss seeing your Mr. Doctor this summer," said Michael. "Shall I drop by his office on your behalf? Give him an update?"

Michael isn't enough for you.

I couldn't let go and I didn't know why.

The quarry water was flat, the breeze had disappeared. I loved being in the water. Yet today, I had to work up to diving in. Too much to think about.

I ran my fingers through raindrops on the dock bench and began to spell: *river of hands.* Where had I heard that before? I fingered another word: *nervosa.*

He'd told me *nervosa* meant "nervous" but only in Latin. It had no real definition in the English language. How could something be real and not exist?

"The word also describes a trunk or treelike pattern of veins within the leaves," he'd said. "*Psychotria nervosa* has beautiful, bright-green leaves."

Mom loved growing things. *Dry as pitch*, she used to say. I closed my eyes. Was my life a pattern I couldn't see? Suddenly, these words came shooting through me: *Dive in. Turn to water before it freezes.*

"There you are," said Dad, stepping down the dock stairs. He rubbed the stubble on his chin and looked up at the grey sky. He was wearing yellow swimming trunks, a recent gift from Linda. She was always giving him gifts. "You look like a banana," I wanted to say but didn't.

"Geez, that was a deep sleep." He made a clacking sound with his tongue. "My mouth is so dry." He noticed my pop can and smiled. The skin beneath his eyes was rimmed with dark circles despite his sleeping in. *Bad dreams?*

"You hate Diet Coke, Dad."

He grabbed the can and downed the contents in one long gulp.

The Watch

I FOUND A PLACE OFF-CAMPUS to rent for my final year, a basement apartment. No more residence life or sharing a dorm room with "Room Service." Real furniture from a real house, though not my house or home. I would learn how to make it my home.

Mrs. Cohen, my landlady, was a twiggy woman with sparrow-like eyes. She watched the three of us unpack the Malibu and the Caddy from her side window, her head poking between the gauzy curtains.

"That her?" Dad said, carrying in another load.

"Yeah." I followed him down the stairs.

"Tell her you need brighter bulbs. It's too dark down here."

He stooped and sneezed from the mothball smells. "It's like being inside your mother's cedar chest," he said, wiping his nose.

"Some flowers and air freshener," said Linda, standing beside him. "It'll be fine." She handed him a Kleenex.

Linda didn't tilt her body toward Dad the way Mom used to whenever she stood next to him. In all the photos I remembered, Mom angled her hips to accommodate his one-leg-longer-than-the-other slant, so it looked like they were standing on the edge of something, a ramp or slope, instead of a flat surface.

"Where is that boyfriend of yours? Some help he is." Dad stood in the middle of the kitchen, filling it up, his body bent like a coat on a hook.

"He's working, Dad. He's at the restaurant. I told you already. Don't you listen? He tried to change his shift." I'd hardly seen Michael this past summer, but he called often. When he did come to the quarry, he slept in Nana's old room. The adjoining bathroom made it easy for us to snuggle there. Michael wanted more, and even though Dad slept with the TV on, I couldn't relax knowing he was nearby.

I worked long hours and had taken few days off the past few weeks—I'd lose too much money. Michael wasn't happy. "We'll see each other soon," I'd said last night on the phone. He'd drop by my new place after work, after Linda and Dad had left.

Dad eyed the stairs we'd just climbed down. "How 'bout that? You've got no door."

I put down Mom's scale in the corner of the closet-sized bathroom. I had to tilt it against the wall to make it fit. "Of course I have a door. It's how we got in."

Dad took hold of my arm and led me back upstairs. "See?" He pointed to the door that led to Mrs. Cohen's portion of the house. "She has her own door, but you don't." He rattled the screen door that led to outside. "She can walk in from here and see you down there." When we looked down, Linda waved up at us. She looked silly waving. "Things to think about before you sign a lease," he said, waving back at Linda. "But no. She has to do things on her own now."

"DARK PLACE," Michael said after checking out the small rooms – bathroom, kitchen, bedroom.

"Of course it's dark. It's nighttime." I opened the fridge, the inner light glared. "Want one?" I said, lifting a can of Diet Coke. Linda and Dad had left hours ago, and I was getting used to being alone.

He sniffed at the Diet Coke. "Stuff's bad for you, you know."

"Oh, and like Equal's good for you."

"You're right, I should stop using it, but I like my coffee sweet." He opened a kitchen cupboard. "You need food. I'll take you shopping tomorrow. No classes till Wednesday, right?"

I opened the can and sipped the fizz. "I have to go to the Psych Building tomorrow," I said, avoiding his eyes. I took another sip.

He leaned against the fridge and folded his arms.

"What?" I said, squeezing the can, the aluminum crinkling.

"What do you mean *what*? I thought we could do something special to start the new term." He chewed his lower lip. "It's your dad again, isn't it? You know I had to work. I tried to change today's shift."

"I know that, Michael. It's okay." I touched his shoulder. "I know you wanted to help."

He slipped his arms around my waist and pulled me in. "You're tired and so am I. I'll stay over another time." He reached for his bomber jacket on the coat stand.

I was glad he was leaving. I wanted to look well and rested tomorrow. I wanted to look pretty. "Thanks," I said as I followed him upstairs.

He turned on the last step and just stood there staring down at me. "For what, Caitlin?"

I should've said then how I really felt. *This isn't working. You're not enough for me.*

AFTER HEARING MY KNOCK at the half-open door, three quick taps, Dr. Delio looked up from his computer and smiled. "You're back."

I closed the door.

"You look well," he said, and motioned for me to sit on the chair beside his desk. "I had a feeling you'd drop by today. So, how was your summer?"

"Okay. Sold bus tours, went swimming..." *Missed you.*

"And how's your dad? Still with Linda?"

I nodded and winced.

"A younger woman's not uncommon, you know." His eyes crinkled when he grinned. "She'll be good for him. She'll keep him young." He flicked through some papers. "One more thing here and I'm all yours."

I sat back in the chair. My chair. Can you stay young by being with someone younger? No doubt Dad was eating more salads, less steak and greasy fries. He was more active too, with daily walks and weekend bike trips, but dock time was still our time. "I don't talk to Linda like this," Dad had said to me several times this past summer. I felt special then.

She was in his life, but she was not his life. Not like Mom used to be.

Dr. Delio's office hadn't changed since last spring. Scattered books and stacks of papers lined all the flat surfaces, including the windowsill. When I turned to the filing cabinet, I saw the mouse I'd given him, one of Mom's Quarry Craft mice, my leaving gift. Smaller than the bride on my bedroom dresser at the quarry, a third of the size. She must've sat there all summer, a little piece of Mom from me.

She'd made this mouse from the same fabric she used for her homemade makeup box. The year before Mom died, she wore the most makeup she'd ever worn. As soon as Nana had her settled in her chesterfield nook, Mom's beauty ceremony began. Foundation. Powder. Blush. Lipstick. She never bothered with eyes, barely an eyelash left to lash. Gone like the athletic muscles in her body. But she could still sew. Fabric purses like that fabric box and those finger-sized mice. They soldiered the shelves of our family room. Little sentinels dressed in puffy skirts and calico hats, black threads for whiskers, tail poking out like an afterthought. Her hands became her voice. Doing and making, her method of communication. Whenever I touched something she'd made—a calico mouse, the green gingham patchwork quilts in my bedroom—I was touching the language of her hands. I was feeling myself back into her.

He opened his daybook. "We'll start your independent study next week. Tuesday good? I'll take you through the lab. How about two?"

"Two."

Me. You.

AT THE END OF THE WEEK, I drove back to the quarry, day-dreaming about next Tuesday. What I'd say. What I'd wear. I was glad Michael had to work all weekend. He wouldn't want to celebrate Dad's birthday anyway. I turned on the radio and pushed the buttons to find the right song to day-dream about Dr. Delio.

I had Mom's car now, thanks to Linda. "It's just sitting there, Don. She can handle highway driving, don't you think?" To my surprise, Dad had handed me the keys the night before I left for my Bond Street basement apartment. "Take good care of it," he said. Was this a sign that he was letting me be more independent? The car was Linda's idea, but he didn't say no. He could've said no.

I moved to the passing lane and accelerated past the slow-moving cars. *I'll tell Michael I need some time on my own when I get back. I just won't use the word* breakup. I rolled the window down further to feel more blasts of air across my face.

When I arrived home, Dad was drinking a bottle of Labatt's on the dock, an empty one beside him, the gas lawn mower sitting in silence, his lawn cutting complete. The scent of cut grass weaved through the soft breeze. He was lying on his lawn chair in his suntanning pose, only the sun was too weak to penetrate skin. No doubt QT was doing the trick. He told me he was going out to Buffalo with Louie that night and that we'd celebrate his birthday tomorrow. He wanted Linda to come with us. We hadn't been to Chef's in a while, not since the middle of the summer, during a night of cele-bration when I'd sold enough tickets to fill a whole bus. No mention of Michael. This time I didn't mind.

"Grounds look nice, Dad." I breathed in the fresh smell.

"Yup. Got my workout doing that," he said, not opening his eyes.

Sweat trickled down the creases of his forehead. His face baked like earth. September's weather seemed an extension of summer.

"This," he said, opening his eyes, fanning his arms, "is yours. The land. The water."

I sat at the edge of the dock and dipped my hand, watched the glitter of sunfish rise to the fake bait. "Even the fish?"

He smiled and folded his arms across his chest. "Even the fish. I mean it," he said. "I've made a will. And if anything should happen, I want to be buried beside her."

"Why are you talking like this?" I hugged my bare knees. The water trickled down them.

"You need to know. I needed to tell you."

I thought of the grey granite stone at Greenwood Cemetery, Owen Sound, the Maharg family plot that sat below a row of sky-high maples. The name *Mary Ellen Maharg* engraved below her father's name: *Captain Roderick Maharg.* He died before I was born. I recalled Mom's pointing finger whenever we drove over the Burlington Skyway to visit Aunt Doris and family, before the falling-out. We'd see Mom's father's old freighter docked in the harbour, *The Shirley G. Taylor.* As captain of a Great Lakes ship, he embarked on long commissions and left Nana doing everything – keeping house, raising children, living a widowed life.

"Will we go there?" Hard to believe another year had passed. "We haven't gone since –"

"Before it snows," he said. "We'll go, don't worry."

I felt safe and warm there with Dad behind me. We were getting through the grief.

We sat in silence after that. The water flat like a layer of glass you could lift. But I knew that sight was an illusion, a trick of the eye. And then these words rose through me, up through the blood from the marrow of my bones: *Be careful tonight, Dad.* I squirmed with the urge to say them, but when I turned, his blue eyes brimmed with calm.

THEY CAME THAT NIGHT. No. They came early the next morning. When Linda arrived, Constable Packer was outside Dad's study window beside his OPP car flashing red, red, red.

"I didn't want to leave her alone," I heard him say to Linda through the window screen. *Alone.* That word in me now. Feet up, knees to my chest, tight like a container. I rocked on the pullout couch in a room filled with his things. *Be careful tonight, Dad.* The unsaid words. And now he was dead.

"What happened, officer?" said Linda.

"Vehicle skidded and flipped — landed upturned in the ditch, east side going north on Stonemill Road."

"Stonemill... One road from here."

"That's right, ma'am."

"Don never wore his seat belt. It hurt his back."

"It hurt more than his back now, ma'am."

A foot shuffled the gravel.

"What happened?"

"Could've been a deer and he swerved to miss it."

"Yes. Don's seen deer there."

"Just the same, there'll be an autopsy next week."

"Next week. What day is it, officer?"

"Saturday, ma'am. Ma'am? You okay?"

At some point, Michael arrived. After flicking on the study light, he sat down beside me on the pullout couch and put his arm around me. "It's okay, Caitlin. You'll be okay." He left the room and returned with a glass of water. "You need it. Please. Drink."

The substance was cold and heavy in my mouth. It hurt to swallow. When he put his arm around me again, I pushed away. I needed to rock. But when he shimmied away, I wanted him back again. I wanted to feel his body beside me.

"Linda's making coffee. Will you drink some coffee?" His eyes shifted to a presence at the door.

Dad?

No. It was Linda.

"Here you go," she said, handing me a mug.

I took the handle of Dad's favourite coffee mug: *Old tennis players never die they just lose their balls.*

Michael and Linda took over the task of making phone calls, informing loved ones and friends. *Yes, we're in shock. Such a tragedy. She's doing okay. Thanks for your concern.* But there was one phone call I had to make.

"Nana, it's me."

"This is a surprise. You're lucky to catch me. I'm on my way to church."

I took a deep breath. "Dad died last night, Nana. He died in a car accident." I took another deep breath.

"Oh, my."

"I wanted you to know. The funeral's on Wednesday. Visitation, Tuesday."

"What kind of accident?"

"Car."

"That Caddy—"

"He swerved to miss a deer. He saved a deer." I stood up from his desk chair to say this. The telephone cord tightened as I headed to the pullout couch. I couldn't reach it, so I leaned on his study chair, the smooth, cool back of it.

"You're not alone?"

"No. Michael's here. And Linda."

"Linda?"

"His friend."

"Hmm. Yes, always a friend." The suck and click of her gold tooth. "Daytime accident?"

"No. Night."

"And the car?"

"Impounded."

"I suppose he wasn't wearing a seat belt."

I wrapped the cord around my wrist.

"No need to answer. I'll be there," she said. "I'll cancel activities."

"I'll see you, Nana."

"Yes. See you, dear."

I stared at the receiver, the tiny holes. *His voice went through here.* I pressed the phone to my ear.

I WALKED DOWN THE AISLE of the crowded church to the front pew and wedged between Michael and Nana. Linda had retreated since Nana's arrival. Respectful? Nervous? I couldn't tell. But I'd have them switch places if I could. Linda beside me. Nana at the back.

"Let us pray," said Reverend Barker.

Déjà vu filtered through me. But this was a new death. This time round, I did the casket picking.

"You'll want the model your mother's in," the pudgy funeral director had said when Michael drove us to Thompson's Funeral Home—two days ago? I'd lost all sense of time.

"We want an open coffin." Nana peered into the satin insides, eyeing the gold silk pillow.

"Of course, Mrs. Maharg. We'll see to that."

At the visitation yesterday, I prepared myself to see his dead body. I'd already avoided going to the morgue. Linda and Michael had done that for me. I was grateful for that. I didn't want to see him slotted in like one of the envelopes he kept in his desk drawers. But maybe, by seeing his dead body, I wouldn't be haunted by nightmares like I was after Mom's death. I braced myself as I entered the room – stiff and waxy, still and quiet. But when I looked, the coffin was closed. "His face, even with expert touch-ups, was too bruised for viewing," said the funeral director.

I put my hand on the pew. No bigger hand there to give it a squeeze.

We stood up to sing. A room of mouths. A mass of black-birds. And then I heard his gawky off-key voice. *That can't be true. It's a hallucination.* What my mind wanted, him singing beside me.

It was warm that September day, summer warm, too warm to wear Mom's monogrammed sweater, her last gift to me, what I wore to the last funeral – my first funeral. I fiddled with the ID bracelet and sang the alphabet in my head, but the reverend's words cracked through: "Yea, though I walk through the valley of the shadow of death…"

After the service, we headed downstairs to the basement reception. The church ladies were happy to see Nana. They revolved around her like gossipy children. Same set of faces from the last funeral. Eleanor. Carol. A black reunion.

Cindy. Last time I saw her she was a smaller version of me. Skinny and tiny, before hormones reigned. The sight of her as an adult snapped me out of my haze. She was bigger than me. A large Russian doll, a vessel of flesh, with room for me to fit into.

"I'm so sorry," she said, her brown eyes tearing up.

"Thank you," I said. What else to say?

"Caitlin," said Aunt Doris, putting her arms around me. My body stiffened. I couldn't help it. Someone intervened with a silver tray, a pyramid of crustless white sandwiches. I took a triangle stuffed with egg salad and set it on a serviette. I knew I wouldn't eat it.

Dr. Delio wasn't at the funeral, of course, but I imagined him sitting in his office, wanting to be there. He needed to know, someone had to tell him. He'd wonder where I was. But I couldn't make the call. I was looking out at the quarry, at the whitecaps coming and going, trying to summon the energy to change out of my funeral clothes, when Michael returned from Dad's study after making that call.

"Dr. Delio seems like a nice guy. He's concerned about you. Called it a double tragedy. I guess he knew about your mom."

"Yes." I watched for a sign of jealousy on Michael's face. No hint of it in his voice. *You still have no idea how attached I am to him.* "Anything else?"

"Take your time. Take as long as you need."

I could hear his voice saying those words. I could hear their double meaning.

"I MUST GET BACK to Owen Sound," Nana said the morning after the funeral. She tapped her Samsonite suitcase. "Meals on Wheels to take care of."

"Let me help," Michael said, grabbing the handle.

We walked her to her car. She'd parked the gold Olds-mobile in the Caddy's old spot.

"Things come out," she said, tilting her face, her signal for me to kiss her on the cheek. Scent of talcum on skin. We watched her drive away.

"Piece of work," Michael said. "Things come out."

"Was that what she said?" I'd already turned her words into *things work out*, what Dad used to say.

"It's going to be okay, Caitlin." Michael put his arm around me. "We'll get through this."

Dad had said that, too.

THE NEXT DAY while Michael and I were eating a late break-fast – I'd barely slept through the night – there was a knock at the side door that made me jump. "It's okay, Caitlin. I'll get it."

The dark pain of that night moved through me – the knock at my bedroom door, a badge slipping through the bottom slit of it. I don't know why I'd asked to see the police-man's badge. My bedroom door had no lock. All he had to do was turn the handle, walk in.

"You have my deepest condolences, Caitlin," said Con-stable Packer. His OPP badge flashed from the sunlight slicing through the kitchen window. He fiddled with his hat.

I nodded and leaned on the counter in front of the sink. The plastic bag crackled beneath his awkward hold. "You'll want these, I'm sure," he said, handing it to me.

It was warm, the bag. And when I opened the Ziploc, air puffed out. Tiger eye ring. Gold bracelet. Watch.

The crack of his skull against the dashboard. "Tell her he died with no pain," I'd heard Constable Packer say to Linda. Immersed in her own pain, she'd forgotten to tell me.

Mom died in pain.

I thought the watch would be cracked and useless, but the glass in my hand was smooth. Only the leather strap was smeared with dried dirt. Pieces flaked off when I touched it. I watched them fall to the carpet.

Gold, orange, rust. It was Mom who'd picked the carpet's autumn colours. She'd hated that grey and pasty linoleum underneath. I was with her when she found the pattern. She brought home a sample to show Dad. "A carpet in the kitchen? You sure, Russ?" He hummed and hawed until the sample sat jammed in a corner, forgotten.

Then one day I came home from high school and strange chemical smells oozed from the kitchen. She was standing with her back to the sink. She was taking the new beauty in.

"It finally happened," I said, watching her.

"Yes. Your father loves it." She butted her cigarette in the glass ashtray. "I knew he would."

"You knew all along, didn't you? You didn't bug him about it. I would've bugged him about it." As I stared at the floor, the shapes of the colours turned to autumn leaves, like the leaves on the Niagara Escarpment. October leaves.

The bigger pattern had emerged.

"You couldn't see that from the sample," I said. "You can really see it now."

"Patience," she said. "And timing. Knowing when to push, when not to nag. I could always see the pattern."

Time ticks and memory persists. They knit together like colours in a rug and entwine to form patterns. The unexpected ticking of Dad's watch told me time would never stop. It kept shoving and shoving me forward, and memory kept pressing and pressing me back.

Old Tennis Players Never Die
They Just Lose Their Balls

"YOU WON'T HAVE TO sell bus tours anymore," Michael
said. "You'll have inheritance money." He eyed me in the
rear-view mirror.

I was sitting in the back seat. I wanted to be in the back.
Linda was beside him, contained, quiet. I shut my eyes and
listened to the hum of spinning tires on the busy highway. I
hadn't sat in the back seat since I was a little girl. *Lambie*. The
stuffed animal that went everywhere with me. Her tatters a
tribute to my love. One googly eye missing. Bald patch where
I'd rubbed my cheek. Her neck, thinned, where I'd gripped
her. The stuffing popping out.

Lambie needs help, Mommy. Look!

With needle and thread she'd fixed Lambie's wounds,

until the insides were sealed again. *Lambie.* Something soft to squeeze when I felt sad and lonely.

"She throws out what she thinks is unhygienic," I muttered, "but she saves every goddamn twist tie?"

"What's that, Caitlin?" said Michael.

"Nothing," I said.

All I had was this purse, black fake leather filled with useless stuff—notes with phone numbers of neighbours who wanted to help. *We're here. Call anytime.* What did that mean? Nobody could bring back my father.

The lawyer Linda had suggested was currently unavailable, so we'd taken Louie's suggestion. We'd driven the long way to get onto the highway to avoid the cutting skid marks, the dented grasses, the black, jagged grooves toward the deadly ditch. A photo of the car accident had made it to the front page of the *Niagara Falls Review*. "Don't look," Michael had said, shielding me from it.

Now, here we were, waiting like patients in a doctor's office, on a row of plastic chairs, flipping through old *Time* magazines.

"Caitlin Maharg, Mr. Dixon will see you now," said the straight-backed secretary.

I didn't straighten my back. I plodded behind her. Michael and Linda followed.

Mr. Dixon stood up from a chair behind a desk that took up half the room, a moat to his bald-headed castle, a mahogany river I could not swim.

"Sit, please."

Only one chair was placed in front of him, so that's where I sat; it was half the size of his big leather one. He pointed to the couch jammed against the side wall, low to the ground. When Linda and Michael sat down, their knees shot up.

"Yes," he said. "Sorry for your loss." He tapped the un-opened file. "We've a lot to get through today." The file was thick, a manila folder like the files on Mom's cedar chest in Dad's study. What would I do with all those files?

"I understand there's no will," said Mr. Dixon.

I thought back to our futile search through the house. "Dad said there was."

"If there isn't a will, we need to proceed." He fingered the glossy desktop. I could see his shadow moving through it. He smiled. A gold tooth like Nana's but no sucking sound yet. "Because your mother didn't have a will and the house was in her name, we have that to settle first. And then there's unpaid taxes."

"Taxes?"

"Seems your father avoided filing tax returns. He owes the government a substantial amount."

Owed. The dead can't owe, can they?

"There's something else we need to talk about." He opened the file to a flimsy paper. "According to his insurance policy, because of accidental death, you qualify for double indemnity."

"I told Caitlin that," Michael said. "I thought that would happen."

"There's a...but...though, isn't there, Mr. Dixon?" said Linda.

"Remind me again of your connection, Miss –"

"It's Ms. – Ms. Walker. I was a close friend of Don's." When she crossed her legs, her body sank even lower. She pulled herself back up.

"Ah, not a family member, so no money then. For a moment I thought we had more surprises on our hands.

And you're the boyfriend, right?"

"That's right," said Michael, his jaw clenching.

"Best to call a spade a spade." Mr. Dixon held up the flimsy paper. "These are the autopsy results. They confirm your father was impaired. The legal limit is point oh eight." He put the paper down to finger the middle of it. "Your father's blood alcohol level was more than double that."

"No," I said. "That can't be right. He swerved to miss a deer—" I stared at my clenched fists and felt a pair of hands cup my stiffened shoulders.

"You're right," said Michael, standing behind me. "This is a lot to take in."

I SAT IN THE BACK SEAT, clutching my purse, twisting the black strap. Quiet. We needed the quiet to take everything in. We were on the highway, driving away from the Falls, but the fall was inside me, a rush that would not calm.

Be careful, Dad. Unsaid words. Words that never hatched, that sat rotten in an abandoned basket.

"It's my fault."

"Caitlin," said Michael, "don't do that. It's not your fault. Your father was drunk."

"Don't say that."

"Michael's right," said Linda softly. She turned to the back seat, but her seat belt pulled her back. "He was drinking heavy lately. The last time we were in Buffalo, I had to take the car keys away from him."

"You did?" I said. "Why didn't you tell me?"

Michael gripped the steering wheel. "No seat belt. Drinking and driving. Look what he's putting you through." He pulled the car into the driveway. The gravel crackled our anger.

"You're judging him," I said.

"Judging him? It's what he did. Otherwise, you wouldn't be in this mess. No will. Need I go on?"

I thought of the lightning bolt sticker Michael had stuck on the bottom of his bedroom door, his symbol of childhood anger at his father. I thought about the bottom of my bedroom door, the *Special* sticker, a discount stamp. And then I remembered my dream: me, the deer, and a car moving through me. And then the deer in the goldenrod field. My lips mouthed what I'd said then: *Mom.*

"You never liked him," I said when the car engine stopped. I pushed the car door open. It whacked the carport beam. I didn't care. I didn't bother to shut it or check to see if I'd made a dent.

I headed straight for the house, for the pullout couch. I needed to sit and cradle and rock, but when I unlocked the door and stepped into the kitchen, I saw his mug sitting upside down in the sink. *Old tennis players never die they just lose their balls.* I picked it up by the handle, took a step back and whipped it fiercely at the window, at the view of the white-capping quarry.

Fragments flew — over the counter, the carpet. They mixed with the autumn mosaic like Dad's watch dust. The mug's words split into letters: *n-v-s* But the *die* was preserved like the window with the view that wouldn't break.

A Wound on Top of a Wound

WE LEFT THE MALIBU at the quarry. I wasn't fit to drive.
Michael had classes to catch up on and so did I. It was hard
to care about getting good grades, too many things to do after
the death of a father. Not as many after the death of a mother.
That's just order and timing of loss. *You're an orphan now.*
Decisions about the house would have to wait, as would what
to do with their belongings. Dead people's stuff.

They'd driven his body to Owen Sound, housed him in
the limestone mausoleum – where Mom's body once rested,
before spring's thaw. We needed to set a burial date. Another
item for the to-do list.

Back on Bond Street in my basement apartment, I was
away from the reality of all that had happened. I had things
to return to – school books, clothes, trinkets. I was safe in

the damp underground with little light coming through. Yet the space that I lived in did not reflect me – mahogany bed, scratched-up dresser. A mismatched set, though under the basement's dim light, it was hard to tell – dark things merged together, and the dresser's mirror held a cloudy sheen, a permanent shroud for my face.

Tell her to take as much time as she needs.

Did he sense I was near? I hadn't made an appointment, but today was our day.

It felt good walking the familiar route again – past the red brick houses along the winding Westdale streets, into the tree-filled campus. Yellow and red leaves fell like sporadic rain in the gusts of wind. Crackle of anger beneath my feet. Senses. I had my senses to take things in, to tell me I was alive.

I took the long way round, walked through the Gothic archway of University Hall. The thick green leaves had sharpened to the ripeness of red apples. I walked through the arch of cool stone, made myself believe I was entering a new world.

His door was open. I didn't have to knock. My heart whirled like a windblown leaf.

"Caitlin."

The sight of him turned me animal-still.

"Come in," he said.

I couldn't move. I froze in the doorway until I felt a bracelet of warmth around my wrist. He guided me to my chair. It was hard to see through my welling eyes.

His caring expression made the tears flow. And then I heard a gasp so deep and guttural I couldn't believe it came from me. Sheltered by his eyes, he let me talk. So I did. Day by day I told him about the deer that Dad swerved to miss, the guilt I felt from not stopping him that night, how it gnawed and gnawed at my insides.

"The deer — remember my dream? I knew... I could've stopped him."

"You didn't know, Caitlin. You had a dream, but you didn't know." His brown eyes glistened. "Please don't do this to yourself. You have to stop this."

"I'm not sleeping. I can't sleep."

"Grief takes on many forms — sleeplessness, anxiety, loss of appetite. Caitlin, your feelings aren't good or bad. They're your basic emotions. They help you navigate through life." He flicked the blind to bring in the remains of afternoon light.

Basic emotions. I thought back to the list I'd memorized in his class: *anger, disgust, fear, joy, sadness, surprise.* "Sometimes I don't feel anything."

"That's okay."

"It doesn't feel okay."

"Is someone pressuring you to talk? Michael? Your Aunt Doris? Your grandmother?"

"Nobody's pressing me. I mean, pressuring me."

He swivelled in his chair. Our feet hit.

THE HOUSE NEEDED an alarm system. Sitting vulnerable and empty, it was easy prey in its uninhabited state. Who would help me? Michael. I needed Michael.

But the hole in my body continued to refuse him. My inner thighs clenched. I let my mouth or hands do the work. I didn't care if he reciprocated. I could do that myself. With two losses, I had an even bigger excuse for what was closed to him.

"We need to get rid of the liquor and beer and hide the hi-fi equipment," said Michael. "TV's old, it should be okay. You'll want to hide these antiques, too." He waved his arms and pointed. "All these windows make for an easy target." He lifted the ruffle of Mom's homemade curtains. "They look nice, but they do nothing. What you need are blinds."

I nodded to show I was listening. Only half of me was. The other half was in a third-floor office.

"We'll need to set a burial date." Michael looked out the family room window at the push of grey cloud. "Weather's turning."

"I know. I will." *Will.* Hard to say that word. Why would he lie?

"Bills to pay. Grounds to take care of. We've a lot to do this weekend. Midterms coming up."

"Why bother? Let the grass grow."

"You're kidding, right?" He pulled at the hem of his Wham! T-shirt. "Your dad would turn in his grave if he heard you say that. These grounds were his baby."

"Only after Mom died. Only then did he get so anal." *Messy widower turns fussy.* "Maybe it's time I did the opposite." *Fussy orphan turns messy.* "And he's not in a grave, he's in a moratorium."

"Mausoleum."

"That's what I said."

"You need a drink. I'll make you a drink."

"Yes. And then let's go driving. I'd like to hit a deer."

He stopped fiddling with his T-shirt. "I don't get you, Caitlin. Maybe you need to see someone. Talk things out."

"I am seeing someone."

"You are?"

"You know."

"He's a counsellor, too?"

"Yes." *There. I'd said it. Proof I could stretch the truth. Bravo. You are your father's daughter.*

"Well, if he's not helping you, maybe you need to see a real counsellor."

"What makes you think he's not helping me?"

"You just said."

"I didn't say that, Michael. Can't you hear me?"

I told Michael to go into town without me to purchase the alarm system. Alone in the car, he could drive the quick way. He could pass the black skid marks I couldn't pass.

I sat down on the chesterfield, curled up my legs and looked out the window. The waves mesmerized, like the way an electric fan dulls extraneous sounds, a lull that led to a core of deep stillness, to the centre of the whole.

At that moment, I knew why Mom loved sitting here on her perch of silence, looking out at the oncoming waves. Waves were like thoughts, rolling and soothing thoughts, healing.

I'd been told the quarry water turned beneath the ice. When the frozen surface loosened, it would honeycomb and candle and tighten to black, absorbing the sun. Then the water would push its way up and tunnel the top layer. The switch natural and right.

When I closed my eyes, an image appeared. It was the drowned woman, her bloated body rising from the depths, her long hair waving like underwater weeds.

I CLIMBED THE three flights and crossed my fingers. Will he be in? *He.* I still couldn't say his name. When I heard his voice down the hall, I slowed my pace. Is he on the phone?

No, not anymore. The comforting click of the keyboard. I stood in the doorway.

"Caitlin, come in. This is a surprise." He lifted the books from my chair. "You have something new to tell me. I can see it on your face."

I sat down on the chair and tucked my knees up, wrapped my arms around them.

He leaned forward and lowered his voice. "You can tell me anything. You know that."

"Yes," I said, tightening the hold, interlocking my fingers. "She doesn't want him buried there."

"Your grandmother?"

"She phoned on the weekend. She left a message on the machine. She would've heard Dad's voice. We haven't changed the message yet."

"Oh my. We?"

"Me. Michael. We were at the house doing stuff."

"Doing stuff, yes." He raised his arms over his head. They looked like wings. Dark with sweat spots. I felt the urge to unlock my arms and nestle there. "What did she say?"

"She was confused by a phone call from Greenwood Cemetery. They wanted to know what to do with the body."

"He's there?"

"Yes. In the moratorium—I mean mausoleum. He wants to be buried beside her. He told me that day on the dock." I uncurled my legs and stamped the floor. I needed to feel something solid. "I can't let this happen. I won't let this happen. She wants money too. She says she lent Dad money to help with Mom's home care. She wants it all back, and the dolls and the dishes, and we don't have those. She's making that up."

He passed me a Kleenex. "Why would she make that up? Have you talked to her yet?"

"I wanted to, but I was too upset. Michael stopped me."

He touched his beard. "Try writing her a letter. Get it down on paper first. See what you have to say before you say what she'll listen to. Do you understand, Caitlin?"

"I don't know," I said, wiping my eyes.

"I got this for you. Here."

The cover was the colour of marsh, the paper edged with gold. I blinked to stop seeing the vision of Nana's gold tooth.

"Give it a try. We can discuss what you've written later if you like."

I took his gift and caressed the journal's smooth leather cover.

"It's trauma, Caitlin. You've experienced the deepest wound – a wound on top of a wound."

On the walk back to my basement apartment, I clutched the journal and thought of the word *wound*. How it spells "wound" as in *bound, pound, found*. I needed both of them in my life, and I didn't have to choose. I was in limbo like my father in the mausoleum's limestone dark. I watched the leaves fall and felt the soft ground freeze over. Too late to bury him now. The winter would shield me from confronting Nana.

"GOOD TIMING," he said when I reached the third floor after taking the stairs. He flashed a white card, and the metal door clicked open. I followed him into a room crammed with stacks of metal cages. I could hear the soft rustle of scurrying feet. The stench of urine and stale woodchips permeated. He handed me a white lab coat.

"First you check for plugs," he said after putting on a pair of latex gloves. He lifted a female mouse by the scruff of the neck and turned her over. The pink nub between her legs was rumpled, the sign she was pregnant. He turned her round, pinched her skin through her thick fur and stabbed a needle through the skin tent he'd created. "Epinephrine. Fight-or-flight drug. Your turn."

The first mother-to-be squirted from my hand. I aimed for the scruff and held on. Her legs scurried in the air. She pooped.

"They do that, I'm afraid. Another reason for gloves." He handed me a fresh needle.

I shifted the hanging mouse to my other hand. She continued to wriggle.

"Grip a little harder."

She stopped squirming.

I wasn't squeamish. I wasn't afraid of needles, but I'd never administered a needle like Mom did during her nursing days. I recalled the black and white photo in Nana's living room, a headshot of Mom in her nursing uniform, the look on her face, gentle but knowing. This task would be old hat to her.

"Excellent! Well done, Caitlin." He patted my shoulder. "Hard for most girls. Some faint."

It felt good to be good at something Mom did. No, that wasn't quite right. Mom's injections helped. Mine were damaging. And her cancer-riddled body was a pincushion for punctures.

The drugged and pregnant mouse sped to the corner of the cage. She flicked manically through the pile of woodchips as if looking for what had been taken from her. Once all the mice had given birth, we'd compare the litter sizes with the control group's, see if the stress hormone, epinephrine, had made significant results.

When I left the lab, I felt a fresh moistness inside me. His hand on my shoulder, our shoulders touching, the smell of musk from the rough of his neck. The lab's close quarters had wired my senses. I checked my watch. Michael would be waiting.

He was standing outside my basement apartment. He followed me in. I turned to kiss him, and while kissing him, I guided him down to the kitchen floor and unzipped his jeans. I undid mine. We were in the middle of the kitchen when I straddled him. In. I put him in. He eased through the moistness, and when I closed my eyes, he began to moan. I could hear my landlady moving above us, the soles of her tiny feet.

Because he came so fast, the pain inside me was quick, like a knife nick. Whom I imagined beneath me had made all the difference, a long, lean body sporting a trim beard.

"That was beautiful, Caitlin." He stroked the length of my arm, my dishevelled hair. "I love you."

"Yes," I whispered, closing my eyes to stop the tears.

Figure and Ground

WE WERE DRIVING UP Windmill Point Road to the quarry,
up the slope to cross the railway tracks, when I felt the sudden
urge for Michael to accelerate. *If a train had been coming, I
wouldn't have stopped.* That day with Darren seemed so long
ago. If a train had been coming, I would be dead. I wouldn't
have to go through this. The white clapboard farmhouse
across the entrance to our driveway had come into view,
boarded and abandoned, where Brenda used to live. Where
was she now? I had no idea.

Did I want to know? Our lives had intersected the
summer I was a lifeguard because I needed her there. Companion. Co-pilot. Someone to accompany me on my nightly
journeys back to Hideaway Park to see Darren, to be alive
in the glow of his American eyes. But was his wanting me

the only reason I wanted him back? A natural reciprocation for his arrow of intent? Darren, a stoner who lived in Buffalo on the wrong side of the tracks, a few blocks from Chef's Restaurant.

"Nothing lasts," I said as Michael dodged another pothole on the gravel driveway. Dad used to fill them in.

"What?" said Michael, hitting one. The car bounced before recovering from the dip. "Don't get what you're saying, Caitlin."

"Doesn't matter," I said. "Neither do I."

When he drove round the bend, I saw the quarry, the puzzling oval of rippling blue.

ONCE INSIDE THE HOUSE, I began sorting through their belongings—what to keep, what to donate. Categories helped diffuse the cloud of chaotic feelings. This goes here. That goes there. Perhaps now we'd find the will, proof that Dad hadn't lied to me that day on the dock. Perhaps one did exist.

I gathered the files from Dad's study to pass on to Mr. Dixon. Tax stuff. The remaining files contained information about Dad's former clients. I dumped them into the garbage bag. And then I found a file within a file, packed with Dad's spidery script, pages and pages of yellow foolscap.

"I don't believe this," I said, flipping through the loose papers.

Michael stood at the study door. "What is it? The will?"

I handed him a sheet and watched him as he read it.

"Shit. This poetry his?"

"Yes." I dropped the papers with Dad's messy handwriting on his desk and headed for the pullout couch. I didn't fold myself in and rock like a baby. I didn't feel the need to rock.

Michael put the sheet on top of the other yellow papers and sat down beside me. I leaned into his shoulder. I tried not to imagine a broader shoulder.

He went back to the study closet. "There's more boxes back here, did you know that?" He pulled out two.

A box like a cube, a box like a doubled coffin.

He didn't have to open them. I knew what was inside: the antique dolls and the Blue Willow dishes.

WHEN I ARRIVED AT HIS OFFICE, he opened the window. Cool air slipped in and my news slipped out.

"Dad hid them from her. He kept them for me. What should I do?"

"Your grandmother gave them to your mother when she was sick."

"Yes. When she came to live with us."

He shook his head. "My, my... And you thought your grandmother had taken them."

I was still trying to adjust to this latest revelation. The dolls and the Blue Willow dishes hadn't disappeared with Nana. They'd disappeared because of Dad. He'd hid them for me. "And she wants money. I told you that, didn't I? Money she gave my parents to help with Mom's home care. Can you believe her? Anything to do with Dad drives her crazy, and I embody half of him. But I'm half of Mom, too. It's as if she can't see that half."

He leaned back in his chair. He did this to think, to reach a conclusion. "Sometimes we choose our perceptions without knowing it. The mind can be calculating, deliberate. Remember the two faces and vase?"

"The dual images? We did that first year."

"You could see both forms immediately, couldn't you?"

"Of course."

"My guess is your grandmother lacks that ability. Her mind would settle on the two faces or the vase."

I looked out the window behind him. The view to the escarpment was blocked by a row of tall brick buildings and thickly branched maple trees. Dark-boned skeleton trees. Hard to believe they were alive inside.

"Black and white thinking, you mean."

He nodded. "How are things going with the lawyer now?"

"He wants to know what I want to do with the house, the quarry."

"And? Any thoughts?"

"I don't know. He's still sorting out Mom's side of the estate." I closed my eyes to see the quarry. "And yet," I said, opening them.

"What is it, Caitlin?"

I saw us living there. Sitting on the dock. Watching the sunset.

ACCORDING TO the brothers Grimm, Linda should have been someone I hated. But Dad's death released a new path for us, a chance to begin anew, to get to know one another, without his awkward orchestrations.

She was sitting at our table at the back of the Westdale Diner when I walked in. We'd been meeting there for weeks now, a five-minute walk from my basement apartment. The wrinkles had deepened on her face, that line between her green eyes — long like an exclamation point. She'd been so calm throughout all of this, but perhaps calm was another form of shock.

It was during these weekend lunches that we began giving each other pieces of the person we'd lost, pieces of his life no one else could give us. The stories that passed between our refilled cups of coffee, our soup of the day and our chicken wrap sandwiches brought Donald Maharg to life again.

She told me about the time they went to a bar in Buffalo along the Elmwood Strip. They'd gotten hold of the last two stools at a popular wine bar on a busy Saturday night, and while waiting for their drinks, Dad started to tap the tube of brass casing that ran along the edge of the bar as if it were an instrument. Linda followed suit, and then Dad nudged the woman on his other side to start tapping, and when she started tapping, she nudged the man beside her, until all of the people along the bar were tapping the rhythm Dad had created.

Sometimes we talked about a shared memory. A memory came back to me of a summer evening, the three of us at the quarry — me, Dad and Linda. Linda was already in the water on her way to the floating raft, front-crawling before looking back.

"Water's beautiful," she yelled. "Come on in, Don! Come swim to the raft." Her little kicks sprinkled the water.

Dad was pacing the dock in his yellow swimming trunks. Hands on his back, he kept shaking his head. "Gotta shampoo the hair. Gotta stay close to the ladder." He turned to me. I was sitting on the dock bench, a beach towel over my lap, taking in the last of the day's heat.

"Caitlin," he said, and sipped his beer. "You go in."

So I did. I dove in and front-crawled my way to the floating raft, through the rippling blue and setting sun, the stress of the day, another long day of selling bus tours at Canuck

Motel slipped through my cooling pores. I joined Linda on the floating raft.

She was lying on her stomach, resting her head on her folded arms. I lay down beside her and mirrored her pose. The water droplets from our dripping bodies fell through the gaps of the wooden planks. They made a pinging sound like the end of a summer rainstorm.

"I forgot," Linda said, tilting her head toward me, her wet hair sleek like a second skin. "I forgot he's not a swimmer." She leaned over and whispered, "I hope he's not mad at me."

We heard a loud splash. Dad had slipped off the dock. What he did to get himself completely wet after sitting on the edge with his feet dunked in to get used to the new temperature.

Whenever something inside him signalled *ready*, he'd tip his body toward the quarry and fall in. He was shampooing his hair now, into a snowy tower of creamy lather, masterfully with one hand, his other hand gripping the metal ladder. The tangy blue smell of the Head & Shoulders floated to the raft.

There was a time when I wouldn't have said anything back to Linda after she'd made a comment like that. I'd have let her words dissolve as if I'd never heard them. But there was something in her face that summer day, that open look of worry.

"He's not mad," I said. "Don't worry. And if he is, just ignore him. He'll get over it."

She opened her resting eyes and smiled.

When we turned back to the dock, Dad was already climbing the ladder, the foamy shampoo dissolving in the quarry, becoming part of it. As if sensing our eyes, he stopped climbing midway and swung his body back and forth, howling like Tarzan.

"See?" I said then. "All he wants is to make us laugh."

When I said it again in the restaurant, I said it in the past tense: "All he wanted was to make us laugh, remember?"

Linda smiled at the memory. "Yes," she said. "We sure did laugh."

Sometimes we talked about his childhood. Things he'd told Linda from his boyhood days at Baie-D'Urfé that he hadn't told me. How he and Aunt Doris used to sprinkle carbonic acid on their L-shaped veranda to practise jitterbugging, their moves and slides, and when the song "On the Sunny Side of the Street" began to play at the high school dance, they weaved through the crowd to find one another and danced up a storm.

She knew about his canoe accident, his near drowning, the reason for his staying close to the dock ladder.

"Your Aunt Doris tipped the boat."

"No she didn't. Louie did."

"Louie?" said Linda. "Don said Doris. I'm sure he said Doris."

The sound of Mom's sobs came back to me then. *Maybe you'll come to my funeral.* Those stifled, stuttered sobs in the yellow kitchen before Dad hung up the phone. Dad's comforting arm around Mom's shaking shoulders.

"They didn't come that Christmas," I said to Linda, "but a complete falling-out? They could've come the following year."

She fiddled with her gold hoop earring and said, "Sometimes you push your hurt onto those you love."

Later that night while trying to fall asleep, I thought more about what Linda had said. I thought about Dad and our life at the quarry when Mom was slipping away from us, the constant see-sawing tension between father and daughter, our see-sawing push of hurt and fear.

The following weekend when we met up for lunch again, Linda talked about my mother. Turns out Dad often talked about "Rusty."

"And you were okay with that?" I said. "What did he say?"

She told me the story of how my parents met.

"Your mother was visiting one of her nursing school friends. Hamilton, I think it was. Don was on the road. Or was he living there then? Anyway, he stopped in to have a drink and there was your mother, sitting alone at a table, waiting for her friend. He started talking to her, of course." She smiled.

"I didn't know that," I said.

She looked away from me as if to think. After another pause, she continued. "Don always talked highly of your mother, nothing but good things, unlike your grandmother. Nobody could rile your father up like Florence could."

"I can't believe she doesn't want him buried there."

"She's quite the woman."

"Why doesn't she like him? He never stopped trying to please her, to bring her round."

Linda stared into her coffee.

She asked how Michael was doing. I told her Michael was fine, but I think she knew I was holding something back, so I told her about my confusing feelings (minus Dr. Delio). As much as she adored Michael, she said she understood. She'd felt that ambivalence once. Instead of listening to her intuition, she'd ended up marrying the man.

"I didn't know you were married."

"He took me so far from myself I didn't know who I was anymore."

"You left him?"

"After I found out he was cheating on me." She sipped her coffee. "I blamed her, but I don't anymore. She gave me a way out."

"How long between that and meeting Dad?"

"Oh." She fiddled with her coffee spoon. "Let's see. Six years?"

"You were on your own all that time?"

"It was good—good for me. It brought me back to myself. It showed me I was capable." She shrugged. "I didn't need a man."

"And then..."

"Yes. And then."

"I want to know."

"Caitlin, are you sure?"

"I wouldn't have asked."

She told me it happened the night a colleague suggested they go for a drink at a jazz bar off the QEW, near Niagara Falls. "You know the one," she said. "You pass it on the way to Canuck Motel."

I nodded.

"Karen stayed for the first set and then had to go. She had a husband to get back to. I almost left too, but something made me stay. I felt funny sitting alone at the table, so I took my drink to the bar. I was settling in when this booming voice shouted out a request for 'This Guy's in Love with You.' You know the song?"

"I know the song." *My parents' song.* The song we heard live at the St. Regis Hotel lobby bar. Clearly, Linda didn't know.

"I turned to see who it was, and by then he'd moved beside me to order a drink. 'Nice to be loved,' he said, something like that." Her face softened to the remembered moment. "Funny, I feel a strong connection with your mother because of how we'd both met Don. He was so damn charming. Caitlin, there isn't much more to say."

But there was and I wanted to hear it – until I heard my mother's voice: *Patience. And timing. Knowing when to push, when not to nag. I could always see the pattern.*

THE LAST TIME I injected a plugged mouse, I'd hit bone instead of flesh, neck bone. I wasn't supposed to hit bone. It was important to inject the epinephrine properly.

"Nice work," he said to me.

I'd been given praise but knew I hadn't earned it. The illusion of doing something right, the inherent power in it. Like the illusion behind a magician's trick, the eye believes. So does the ear when it receives a valid story. Especially when the voice sounds like it wouldn't lie. The next time I met Linda for lunch at the Westdale Diner, I·told her about finding Dad's writing.

"Yes," she said, stirring her coffee.

It could've ended like that. Neither one of us would've been the wiser. She said she wanted to go to Toronto to visit the CBC building. She asked if I'd go with her.

"The CBC building? What for?"

She looked at me strangely then. Her everyday face evaporated and an odd quizzical look replaced it. It made me sit back and hit the back of my chair. Turns out the night they met at the jazz bar, Dad had told her he was a writer for the CBC and that he'd soon be taking early retirement.

"I didn't know..." she said after I told her his real job, selling envelopes. "I didn't know he was a salesman."

But he was a salesman even then. Selling lies. Creating an illusion and living inside that illusion. Later, when I adjusted to this shock, the truth of his lie would sadden me more. He never believed he was good enough moving through life as an envelope salesman. What he wanted was to be a writer.

What else did my father lie about?

"He was always so nervous when we were alone together. Did you notice that, Caitlin? When I think about it now, what if you'd mentioned his job? How did he know you wouldn't? And his drinking last summer. Some nights out, he wouldn't stop, couldn't stop – he thought he could handle it. One night it got so bad – I told you this, didn't I? – he wouldn't give me his car keys, insisted on driving. So stubborn... How did your mother deal with that? I wouldn't get in the Caddy until he gave me those keys."

"Dad wasn't an alcoholic. I never saw him drunk."

"Well, he didn't get drunk at home. He drank too much outside the home."

"What do you mean *outside the home*?"

"Bars. Like the jazz bar where I met him. Like that bar in Buffalo he and Louie went to that September night – places he could be who he wanted to be, where he could gather a captive audience."

"The deer. You don't believe he swerved to miss a deer."

"He needed the outlet, Caitlin, but after a few drinks, his personality changed. He became someone different. He couldn't handle the alcohol the way he could when he was younger. I guess it's the side we all have lurking beneath us, the id that wants to come out. I'd like to believe in the deer, I really would. Caitlin?"

"You didn't know him that long. A year at most? He wouldn't do that. He wouldn't mess with his life like that."

That time after consuming too much vodka at Hideaway Park, I'd gotten into the Malibu to drive home. Even in my intoxicated state, I knew not to attempt parking the car in the carport—I'd hit the post. So I left it in the middle of the lane, something I never did, and I forgot about the empty Smirnoff bottle I'd left in the passenger seat. The next morning when I feigned sickness, I received his sympathy. "Not to worry, I'll call Louie for you." But when he saw how I'd parked the car and found the empty vodka bottle, he knew why I was "sick." "Get out of bed right now, Caitlin Maharg, and get to work!"

I put my serviette on the table, pushed the chair back and stood up. "I have to go."

"Is it that late? What time is it?"

"How would I know?"

"Caitlin, honey—"

"He wasn't a drunk. He wasn't. I know my father."

After walking out the door, I realized I hadn't paid for my share of the meal. I couldn't go back in there. Not now. And if I went back to my apartment, she'd soon be looking for me.

I headed down a side street, away from sounds of traffic and strangers' voices, away from pounding noise. I told myself to breathe. Didn't he say that the last time I sat in *his* office? *When you're feeling overwhelmed, remember to breathe.*

I headed down a snowy path lined with full-grown trees and tried to focus on my breathing. The city sounds were distant now. I breathed in rhythm with the windblown pines and cedar bushes, a river-hush sound. A blue jay pierced it with his abrasive cry. I looked up to find it on the high bare branches, but I couldn't see him. The metallic calls continued. I shuddered.

Shut up.

They grew fierce in their frequency. I walked faster to get away from them. Was he following me? When I plugged my ears, I could hear him in my head.

"Stop it!"

Linda was right. Dad didn't drink at home. Only the odd bottle of Labatt's or glass of rye and ginger with Mom. What I did witness growing up when I went upstairs to watch my morning cartoons at the Upside-Down House was this: Dad sprawled on the sectional chesterfield, unshaven, dark circles under his eyes, still wearing yesterday's clothes, his breath minty sour, his skin the scent of Nana's cleaning ammonia.

Valentine

I HAD SOMETHING NEW to tell him, but I couldn't yet.

He got up from his office chair and opened his filing cabinet, reached to the very back and pulled out a bottle of red wine and a pair of wineglasses. "I've been saving this," he said, fiddling with the corkscrew.

Watching him do something I'd never seen him do before helped separate the quicksand in my stomach, the sensation of sinking and floating at the same time. He popped the cork and sniffed. "A Burgundy. Côte d'Or." He poured and passed me a glass. We eyed the ruby liquid.

"To us," he said, and clinked my glass.

"Us."

We sipped.

I was used to drinking warm keg beer or orange juice and

vodka, so it took a few sips for my taste buds to adjust. The warm red trickled through me. I could tell him now. What I'd found this morning in my basement apartment, what had slipped out of Dad's file folder, the one I'd taken back to Hamilton with me so I could try to decipher the handwriting of his poems.

"Now you can tell me," he said.

I pulled the evidence from my knapsack and handed it to him. He eyed the card – the red heart with the piercing arrow.

I sipped as he opened it. His eyes moved to the signature at the bottom before rising to the Hallmark verse. When he finished reading, he looked at me. "You're surprised by this?"

"The date. Look at the date."

He put the card face down on his desk.

"Well?" I said, as if accusing him.

He set his wineglass on top of the card and linked his hands round the back of his head. Blue veins rivered his inner arms. "Well," he echoed, "I'm not surprised."

"You're not?"

He put his arms down. "Look," he said, picking up the glass, "your father loved your mother. Cared for her. Stood by her through the stages of her illness." He looked me in the eye. "Can you deny that?"

"No," I said grudgingly.

"Think about the enormous stress he was under – financing her care, dealing with your grandmother, wanting what's best for you. Did it sound like he was out to meet someone that night?"

"I guess not."

"Chance brought them together. Your mother – she was in her final stages then."

"But it was December when she got pneumonia."

He wheeled his chair closer to mine. "I know this is hard to see right now, you're too close up. Someday you'll see."

"See?"

"It's the most stressful experience a spouse can go through. Linda helped him cope with cancer's horrible ramifications." He took a deep breath. "I tell you this because I don't want you to discount the love between your parents. You saw his grief."

I stared at my glass and let his words decant into me. I felt a touch on my chin. I thought his beard would prickle, but it didn't, that's not how it felt.

THAT NIGHT IN BED beneath the flannel sheets, I replayed that moment. It made my stomach quicksand in a raw, delicious way. Was it cheating? My mind played with this. "I've been wanting to do that for a long time," he'd said before rolling his chair back to see what he'd put his lips to.

After the kiss, we'd sipped more wine. I remembered little else of the evening. A fuzzy, wintery walk to his car, a radio-blaring drive home. He let me out at the end of Mrs. Cohen's driveway. A living room light flicked on as he drove away. The front curtains fluttered. But the kiss was buried deep inside me.

When we lived at the Upside-Down House, I got a weekly allowance of fifty cents. One quarter would go into my piggy bank, the other my pocket. After my morning bowl of Cap'n Crunch, I'd meet up with the other kids my age who lived along the boulevard and the crescent, and we'd all head down to Milk 'n Things.

A quarter could fill a brown bag with penny candy.

Mojos. Black Cats. Licorice Babies. Dubble Bubble. We'd carry our choices like torches to the tall counter and watch the bun-haired lady with the beak nose flick through the bag's contents with her grape-painted fingernails. "Twenty-five cents, right on the dot!"

One Saturday, I put both quarters into my piggy bank. They'd go toward my goal of buying a Ken doll, a boy Barbie. I hated my chopped-haired substitute. Despite my efforts with Mom's sewing scissors, "he" looked like a "she." Those bumps on his chest—nothing could hack those off. Despite not having any money that day, I went along with the others. I stood at the end of the candy aisle and listened to them ooh and aah as they picked out their sweets. But the routine was so thick in me that I thought the beak-nosed lady would think I was stealing, so I purposely walked with my arms spread out and my fingers splayed open, proof I was a good girl.

Where did that come from? The guilt with no locus that ate at my insides? As I lay in bed, I listened to the water running through the pipes behind the wall. Mrs. Cohen's ablutions. I fisted my fingers. A kiss isn't really cheating. It would only hurt to tell.

I WAS COUNTING newborn mice in the lab, prodding the fleshy pink squirms with a wooden stick, separating the litter from the milk-warm mother. Soon we'd know if the epinephrine we'd injected the females with had affected litter size. Adrenalin acts as a stressor, but would it be enough?

The newborns' eyes were webbed with black, such blind helplessness.

Half buried by woodchips lay a pink slice. The head was gone. When I turned around, he was standing behind me.

"Here," he said, holding a Ziploc bag.

I pinched my gloved fingers and took hold of the fleshy stub, plopped it into the plastic sleeve he held open.

"It happens, I'm afraid," he said, sealing the bag.

"Why?" I asked. "She's the mother."

"She knew the runt would die and that protein would provide good milk for her brood." He smiled when he saw the look of disgust on my face. "We animals are a brutal lot."

A blush bloomed through me.

"Caitlin, about the other day—"

"Yes, it's okay."

"You mean a lot to me—I hope—"

"No. I know. It was—"

"A lot to take in."

"Yes. A lot to take."

"Well, good then." He swiped his hands. "We're all sorted."

"We are," I said, sounding more sure than I felt.

"I'll leave you to your data." He wiggled the Ziploc bag. "I'll put this in the freezer."

"Freezer?"

"For the weekly pickup."

As I listened to the beat of his footsteps down the hall, his musk lingered, a living smell.

Vase or Two Faces

HE HELPED ME understand my grief. How my body's shut-down state was a way of conserving energy. Everything had a biological reason, an evolutionary path. He did not believe in God.

"This is our world." He held up his daybook. "The tangibles, the concrete."

"What about things we can't touch, like feelings or hunches?" I squirmed in his office chair.

"They're biological, you know that, Caitlin. They help us to navigate our complex lives."

"You've never believed in God?"

"Never. And you?"

"Dad always said, 'God gives us seven days, the least we can do is give him an hour a week.'"

"God. Another false construct."

"What about Jesus?"

"We need our heroes, our moral men."

"His rising from the dead?"

"A lovely myth like a fairy tale, like *Cinderella*. Wasn't she dead-awakened by a kiss?"

"That's *Sleeping Beauty*."

"The need to propagate is a strong drive. The greater the offspring, the greater the genes' survival."

"Do you mean that's why Dad would choose someone like Linda to be with?"

He smiled.

I wanted to shout, "No, Daniel, that's not why," but I couldn't say his first name like I couldn't say *Dr. Delio*. I had no moniker to fit him.

The ease shifted from his face. His eyes tightened. "You're not upset, are you? I haven't upset you? He may not have wanted Linda to have his child, not in a conscious way." His eyes warmed again. "With a daughter like you, why would he?"

THE LATE-AFTERNOON SUN had disappeared behind a wall of cloud. Streetlights lit my way back to Bond Street. I pulled up my hood to bar the cold.

Long white beard and shepherd's staff. That wasn't the picture of God my mind conjured up. It held a medley of images: sunlight crackling over the quarry water, the wing flap of the great blue heron, a face-to-face encounter with the white-tailed deer. These were the moments that took me out of my fears and concerns, my worries and downfalls, to the stillness that knew no bounds, unearthly moments I felt most human.

Michael stepped away from the maple tree he'd been leaning on. "Where were you?" he said. "I thought we were going to the library."

"I was at the lab," I said.

"Hope he appreciates your grunt work."

I unlocked the apartment door and looked back at him.

"What?" he said.

"It's not grunt work. It's important."

The cold draft followed us downstairs.

"I still don't get what you do."

"What do you mean?"

"Counting mice."

"Litter size. It helps tabulate the effects of the stressor."

"Lovely. So how do things look?"

"Too early to tell, but he thinks the data will be significant. He wants to credit me in the study when it's published."

"*He.* Why do you always call him 'he'?"

I hung up our coats and folded my arms.

He moved to the spot where we'd made love. "What's *he* look like?"

"What does it matter what *he* looks like?"

"I bet he thinks you're cute."

A blush rose through me. I still felt cold.

"How could he not?" He pushed back the hair that curtained my face. He lifted my chin. A mouth prepared to kiss.

"I can't. I have to study."

He kissed my neck. "Shit, you're freezing." He rubbed my arms and looked up at the ceiling. "Doesn't she heat this place?"

"Michael."

"Well," he said, looking straight at me. "At least you say my name."

"Aren't you sick of waiting?"

"What are you trying to tell me, Caitlin?"

"Nothing."

"Right. Nothing."

LYING IN BED THAT NIGHT, the first-year psych textbook on my lap, I stared at the optical illusion: vase or two faces. It was an image with two interpretations—white vase or two black faces—each one valid. But only one was perceived at a given moment due to the shaping effect of figure and ground —fields with a common border. It was impossible to perceive both at the same time, one occluded the other.

Was this what life was like for Dad the months before Mom died? The constant push and pull in two directions?

Part of me didn't want to think about what I was doing. Part of me did. A mind-bender like this eye-bender. I tried to see both at once. I looked away and tried again. I couldn't do it. My mind had to switch. That's how liars compartmentalize. When I'm with Michael, I'm with Michael. When I'm with—

Here, Dad. I made this for you.

He set the bread-dough caterpillar on his study desk, under the cone of lamplight.

Third-floor office. Fabric mouse.

It's not the same.

I slammed the book shut.

A FEW DAYS LATER, I met up with Linda at the Westdale Diner. When I called earlier in the week to make the arrangements, I'd heard relief in her voice. We hadn't talked since my abrupt departure from our last lunch together. Today, we sat at the table we always sat at, only this time I chose the seat facing out.

But now I wished I'd chosen a private place for us to meet. There could be a scene. I could feel the anger burning inside me.

I showed her the valentine card.

She closed the card and passed it back to me.

You can't look at me now, can you? I know who you are. I know what you did. I watched and I waited. I didn't blink. But she did look up and she looked straight at me.

"I'm so sorry, Caitlin."

I thought I wanted to see her squirm, see her face sheet to panic white. Shame. Humiliation. What his wife would want me to do, if she knew about her husband and me.

But that's not what happened when Linda looked straight at me and said she was sorry.

"I know," I said.

She hadn't set out to hurt. We don't set out to hurt.

We pulled tissues from our purses and wiped our eyes. Our food—today's soup—had lost its steam.

I thought back to the story of how they met—at that jazz bar after Dad's request for the band to play his and Mom's song. I thought about his lie—writing for the CBC, what he'd told Linda the night they met. Wasn't that the lie of someone having some make-believe fun? So how did their chance meeting turn into something more serious?

Despite the sensation of another string tightening around my stomach, I leaned forward and said to Linda, "How did he end up seeing you again?"

Linda ran her fingers along her glass of water, clearing the condensation, as if clearing a chalkboard or a messy slate. "He asked for my number, so I gave it to him. Wrote it down on a beer mat. He ripped the written part off and slipped it in his shirt pocket." She paused. "He didn't call that weekend. Not the Saturday or the Sunday. After the weekend, after that first day back at school, I told myself, 'He's not going to call.'

"That Monday night, while I was marking papers, the phone rang. I remember looking at my watch—nine o'clock. I knew it was him. The phone was across from where I sat on the sofa. I put down my papers and listened to the rings: *one, two, three...* I knew I could reach it in one fell swoop, I'd done it before. If it reached seven..."

"Seven," I said.

"Yes, seven."

"The jazz bar again?"

She nodded. "We met there that Friday. He didn't tell me he was married, not that night, but something inside me knew. I just didn't want to face it."

I pictured Mom's life those last months before her death in the hospital on Christmas Day. Their master bedroom had become a mini-hospital. Mom drugged up with injections of morphine, bedridden, flinching with pain, unable to talk or to listen.

"You became his new confidante...what Mom couldn't do anymore..."

"Yes, your father talked—he needed to talk—about what he was going through with your mother, your grandmother. You. He was so proud of you."

"Your psychology classes came in handy then."

"I helped him, Caitlin. I'm not proud of the circumstances, but I know I helped him...and he helped me.

She sipped her glass of water, put the glass down and sipped it again. I sipped my glass. Our throats were dry. Our voices shaky.

I shook my head. "Now we're the ones helping each other," I said.

"Thank you, Caitlin. I needed to hear that."

THE FOLLOWING WEEKEND, I had something else I wanted to ask her. At first, my plan was to tell her about my competing feelings for two men, but that had changed after his recent talk of genes and offspring. It made me ask another question.

"Did you and Dad ever talk about kids?"

"You mean having them?"

I nodded.

She laughed. "God, Caitlin. I'm too old to be a mother."

"No, you're not. You're not even forty." And when I thought further about Linda, I realized she and I were closer in age than she and Dad. No wonder we got along so well. What had Dad called it, whenever Linda didn't do what he thought she should do, or whenever she thought in a way foreign to him — he'd said she came from the "Me Generation."

"That's sweet of you. And I guess you do have a point, but I never wanted children. Teaching's enough for me."

"You've always known that?"

She nodded.

"But how? How can you be so certain? Wouldn't your genes want otherwise?"

"Genes?"

"Procreation. What our bodies are programmed for."

She watched me closely. "Programmed? This doesn't sound like you."

I twisted my serviette. I'd always imagined having a sibling, someone to move through life with, a constant companion, like my cousin Cindy who came to the quarry so many summers ago. Our special dives – the Watermelon Dive, the Scissor-Kick Dive. Someone to share memories with, otherwise they disappeared. But childhood memories had begun to defrost in phrases and fragments. I'd started writing them down in the journal Dr. Delio had given me. The pen-ink fossils of my life.

Turn to Water Before It Freezes

I WENT TO MICHAEL'S THAT CHRISTMAS. His parents welcomed me as if I were a lost member of his family instead of someone they'd just met. His mother was soft-spoken and kind, like my mother, but she didn't act like Mom at all, she wasn't good with her hands, and his father didn't talk about himself to the extent that I thought he would, given what Michael had said. His mother did everything for his father as if doing that defined her. She'd be lost without him. He'd be lost without her. They were locked into a one-sided chain of give and take. I was thinking this when I spotted Michael's lightning bolt sticker on the bottom of his bedroom door.

Linda had given me an anthology for Christmas: *Love and Loss through Poetry*. Between snowy walks along quiet country roads and afternoons of socializing and eating and helping with the cleaning up, I read the book. Moved by the words that moved through me, my insides tinselled like the decorated pine tree in the sunken living room. But I only felt this when others weren't around. I had to be alone for this to happen.

I did not understand this.

Our last night there, I awoke in the middle of the night. The fierce wind that had lulled me to sleep had turned quiet. I could hear the faint crackle from the fireplace down the hall in the sunken living room. The stones that formed the fireplace had been hauled from neighbouring fields and then cut into place like pieces of a giant jigsaw. The light from the fire would be enough.

I slipped out of Michael's double bed, careful not to disturb him, and felt for my journal in the pocket of my suitcase, passed through the dark hallway and stepped down toward the glowing hearth. The flames had waned, but not the ash scent of burnt maple. As I sat on the cut-stone ledge, I pretended I was back at the quarry. When I closed my eyes, I was there.

I couldn't see the words on the page, so I fingered them, the past beneath my fingertips. *This surface for long-legged spiders once absolved teen skin.* I closed the journal and listened to the dying red. I touched my chin. I was warm now. Even my hands weren't cold.

AFTER MICHAEL DROPPED ME OFF at my basement apartment, I found a letter on my kitchen table. The white seal showed a tiny rip. Had Mrs. Cohen opened it? The thought didn't surprise me given our last encounter. I'd just stepped out of the shower, a towel wrapped around me, and was heading for my bedroom when—

"Shit!"

"Caitlin, no need to swear." She'd pulled her key out of a door I had no key for and checked to see if it was locked. "Did I scare you? Didn't mean to scare you." She waved her cellophaned package of meat. "Steak night," she said before heading back up the stairs.

"That's your space," Michael had said when I told him on the phone. "You're the one paying for it."

He was right. Looking back, I must've been saving my energy for a bigger confrontation. I only had so much in me — tired all the time, my jaw in constant ache from the grinding in my sleep.

I opened the letter.

> Dear Caitlin,
>
> I hope you are coping this Christmas. I know this is a difficult time for you.
>
> I thought I'd see you before you left for the holidays. Perhaps you dropped by while I was attending a faculty meeting?
>
> I may have been too forthcoming during our last talk. I didn't mean to make you uneasy. I'm afraid it's the scientist in me.
>
> I miss you.
>
> I'll be in my office the week after Christmas. The door, as you know, is always open to you.
>
> D

What made me see it, clearly, at that very moment, I don't know. *D for Don, D for Dad.*

THEY WENT THROUGH my parents' things. Purses. Plates. Albums. Ashtrays. "This all you got?" they said before moving on to the next table. We priced low because we were told to price low. Still they haggled. But not the nosy neighbours. They weren't there to buy used goods. They were there to see the quarry.

I wanted them all to go home.

I tried to calm myself by singing the alphabet song in my head and letting Michael deal with the hagglers.

"This wig new?"

"Can I try this windbreaker on?"

"Two records for one and I'll take 'em."

Like an invasion of ants, they marched through the bungalow – pick, pick, picking things. Things once held by my parents' hands. Physical remnants of their living landscape, when their bodies pulsed with life and did more personal things like that fat man who'd just farted.

"Mind if I take this?" he said, holding Mom's Zippo, a cigarette jutting from his plump lips.

"Yes," I said, grabbing it back.

His eyes bulged. "Gosh, it's only a lighter," he said, walking away.

I cradled the Zippo in the hem of my T-shirt and wiped off his fingerprints. When I looked down, I saw something else on the table. How could I have missed that? The album with the pleading face. *Please, sir, can I have some more?* Those big eyes brought me back to the Upside-Down House, to that threshold between the living room and the den that served as a stage. I knew each song on the album. I'd practised for hours in my bedroom. But I chose to sing only one song to him.

Is it underneath the willow tree that I've been dreaming of?

A nine-year-old daughter singing "Where Is Love?" to her doting father.

And where exactly was love? I still didn't know. But grief was waiting for a giant black kettle to boil.

"You can't have that album," I said to the frizzy-haired woman holding out a crumpled dollar bill.

"What kind of garage sale is this?" she said.

"Caitlin," whispered Michael, "you were supposed to go through the stuff. I thought you were ready."

The items spread coldly over the makeshift tables proved to be more than just things. They were triggers with tangible memories, the memories of my life. I was losing the cells of myself.

"Tell them to go," I said, grabbing hold of the remaining albums. Burt Bacharach. Ella Fitzgerald. Bing Crosby. Doris Day. Nat King Cole. I stacked them on the upright grand. "Tell these strangers to go, Michael. Don't look at me like that. Tell them now. Do you hear me?"

I CAN'T SAY THAT I knew what I was doing. I can only look back, wedged like sediment between the dead and the living. By the time the winter ice had broken on the quarry and the buried smells had seeped back up, I realized my reactions had done more than create pangs of discomfort. An album you'll never listen to but can't give away, a lighter you keep even though you don't smoke. These reactions were telling me something new about my grief. I was breaking through the numbness.

I recalled what the woman at the garage sale had said to me. I was looking out the window at the time, at the cherry tree Mom loved to watch come into bloom, pink papery blossoms. "I know how you feel," she'd whispered. "I lost my parents not too long ago. Mother died of cancer. Father from a broken heart. You can die of a broken heart, you know."

I turned to look at her. Tall and grey-haired, wrinkled. She wasn't looking at me.

But you're old, I wanted to shout. Death should happen to your parents. Not mine.

The chain of death and family revelations had boiled my world down to this: *What do I have to do to get through the day, and who will help me?*

The wind rolled over the water like a moving bolt of material.

There was something else I had to get through. I flicked the Zippo and watched the flame. I ran my finger through it.

AS A LITTLE GIRL, I was told not to go past the front hedge, the border that lined the long front lawn of the Upside-Down House. I could only peek through the leaves of my green gate. Dad's words, so commanding – *don't you go past or my spies will tell me* – I never dared to disobey him. But I was little then, and now I'd outgrown the hedge. I didn't have to peek through to see past.

I thought I could get through grief like getting from *A* to *B*, like swimming underwater to the floating raft but farther – all the way to the other side of the quarry. The touch of wet rock on my hand would signal: *end.* I would hear: *That a girl!* or *You did it, Caitlin!* And the grief would be over and I would swim back.

But grief wasn't like that. The cause – death – finite. There was no other side to touch and return from, only through and through and through until the water of grief became the water inside you, one and the same, and you took it all in.

Sound Is a Body of Water

WE USED TO COUNT COWS on the drive up to Owen Sound, but when we'd reach one hundred, I'd get bored. Dad liked to comment on the position of the cows – standing up or lying down. One meant rain, the other sun. I could never remember which meant which. "Are we there yet?" My constant refrain. This eventually changed to: "Mom, what town's next?"

Fergus – Arthur – Mount Forest – Chatsworth – names that marked the old Scottish settlements along hilly Highway 6, that signalled the countdown to our final destination.

When I first heard the name of the town Mom had grown up in, I thought it was the name of a boy. Owen. Owen Sound. I imagined his voice. How the sound would permeate like an offshore wind. But *sound* is a body of water.

The dip into town always made me sit up. I'd stare at the flaky layers of moth-grey stone as we made our way down to the town at the bottom, the peopled quarry. Before driving back up to reach Nana's house, on one particular trip we headed to Harrison Park. The place Mom spent her formative years, tobogganing and cross-country skiing, where she learned to play tennis, where she'd escape from Nana's silence.

Once out of the Buick, I fed the ducks the potato chips I'd saved during the long ride up, tossed them over the chain-link fence into the shallow water. Birds came squawking and flapping. I hated the bossy ones, bullies that pinched the necks of the vulnerable. I tossed out diversions, the tiniest bits. *Let them get cutthroat for that.* While they were off nipping at the scraps, I flung bigger pieces to the little ones.

The bossy ducks—they always came back.

Back in Dad's Buick, we drove out of Harrison Park and up the hill to Greenwood Cemetery. After parking beside the limestone mausoleum, we walked through the green fields of headstones, fields of giant teeth, until we reached our family plot. There we stood by the grey granite stone, the chiselled names as foreign as the dates. Only one name conjured up flesh and blood: *Florence Mary Maharg 1905 –*

The first time I read it, I thought she was dead.

Maybe that's why that particular visit, when we finally arrived at her red brick house and I saw her standing on the front step, I dropped my Lambie and ran out of the back seat in my stocking feet, straight into the folds of her flowery apron.

"Oh," she said, her voice loose and airy. I looked up as if to see a star. She smiled down at me. But then she stepped back and the smile left her face and the space grew fat between us.

"She thought you were dead, Mother. She saw your name on the Maharg stone."

"Well." Nana chuckled. "I will be one day. Then again, won't we all?"

And now, here I was, on a hot spring day, having travelled the chain of towns along hilly Highway 6, facing the Maharg family stone again.

I stared at the granite, at my mother's name: *Mary Ellen Maharg.* I recalled the bossy ducks in Harrison Park. How it pays to be pushy.

SHE WASN'T EXPECTING ME, but it was Tuesday, her day of afternoon cleaning after her morning volunteer work at the IODE. I got out of the car, took a deep breath and tucked in my T-shirt, still loosened from the long trip. It was noon, but I walked straight to the back door so she'd hear me knock. I knocked hard. Maybe she didn't have her hearing aid on.

The back door opened.

"Well," she said, "what a surprise." A crumb dangled from the corner of her mouth. She flicked it with the point of her tongue, a little pink animal. "Come in."

One placemat sat on the kitchen table. No eating on laps in Nana's house or, God forbid, in bed, while reading. The whistling kettle startled me, but she didn't see me flinch. She poured hot water into her mug. After dribbling in drops of homogenized milk, she carried it to the table. I thought of Dad's coffee mug: Old tennis players never die they just lose their balls. Nana's mug said nothing. After the kettle's silence, I heard the ticking of the grandfather clock, steady like the heart of something living.

"Sit," she said. "You've caught me in the middle of lunch.

Five-in-One, last night's leftovers. Your favourite." She pointed. "There's some in the fridge."

"No, thanks."

I stared at the row of African violets on the shelf above the kitchen sink. Always there. Always healthy. The ones at the quarry had died after Mom's death. When I turned, Nana was staring at me. Her blue saucer eyes made me straighten up.

"How are you, Nana?"

She swallowed. "I'm well, thank you. We had a lot of snow this year. A lot to shovel off the roof. I'm glad that's over."

"Yes, I'm sure you are."

"And you?" She patted her lips with her serviette. "Have you finished school yet?"

"Almost."

She carried her plate to the sink. Roses on the ties of her apron. I knew the smell of that apron, the scent of time pressed back. Normally, I would sit on the other side of the kitchen table, the sink and window behind me – I was sitting in a new position now, where Mom had always sat.

Nana sat back down and pried the lid off the cookie tin. The smell of sugar wafted up. No Chips Ahoy! in this house. She pulled out two homemade cookies.

"Help yourself," she said, and slid the tin toward me.

She was watching to see what I'd do. No place setting or plate to set the cookie on. I pulled a serviette from the napkin holder.

She nodded. "Will you stay?"

"Stay?" I placed my cookie on the serviette. "I'm not here to stay."

"I didn't think so." She licked her finger and pressed it

over the crumbs on her plate. "Nothing good should go to waste," she said, looking at my uneaten cookie.

"I need some water."

The first cupboard I looked in didn't have drinking glasses. It held dried herbs and spices arranged in alphabetical order: basil, cardamom, cinnamon…the earth smells mingled.

"Over there," she said, pointing. "Don't you remember?"

"Yes." I moved to the other cupboard and pulled out a glass. It was stamped with the face of Billy Bee. I filled it with tap water and sat back down. "Do you know why I'm here, Nana?"

"I can imagine."

Imagine. I couldn't imagine Nana imagining.

"The answer is no," she said.

"No? You don't even know what I'm going to say."

"Don't I?" She set both hands on the table. "Go ahead, Mary Ellen. Ask me."

Caitlin. My name is Caitlin Maharg. I sipped the water and set down the glass. "I'm not going to ask. It's what he wanted. It's what she wanted."

"Oh, to be buried by her husband?" She continued to stare without blinking. How did she do that? "She should never have left him."

"Left him?" I said. "She didn't leave him. She died."

"Just what I thought," she said. "You don't know."

My heart sped up, like Mom's sewing machine, revving and revving, it was revving inside me and I couldn't stop it, Nana's foot pressing the pedal.

"Mary Ellen had a husband, a legitimate husband – Geordie Stewart."

"What are you talking about?"

"Donald Maharg was not her husband."

"No," I said. "He was her husband... They eloped."

She chuckled. "Of course they'd tell you that. Just like your father said he'd give me back my money, my dolls and dishes." She clicked and sucked her gold tooth.

I thought of Mom's maiden name – *Maharg* – how it matched Dad's surname, that connection between them.

"No," I said.

The *no* in my mind turned back to what I'd always known. It slipped into place. She watched me. She was watching this happen to me. *Maharg meets Maharg. They were never married.*

"Sinners."

"How can you say that?" Tears stung. I couldn't see.

But I *could* see. I could see right through her. This was all she had. This was all she had over me.

And now it was nothing because it was out there – no longer locked inside.

"She'll have her wish," I said, standing up. "She'll be ashes and he'll be ashes and I'll scatter them over the quarry." I was leaning on the chair. Could I let go of the chair? Yes, I could.

And when I did, I reached into my pocket. I dropped the cheque on the table, right onto her supper plate. "Eat that, Nana."

Her mouth formed an *O*, and a raw sound came rushing out. But not out of her mouth, out of mine, from the deep core of me. I was laughing.

"Mad," she said, watching me. "Mad as a hatter, just like that Don. Why, the way you're so alike you'd think he really was your father."

I stiffened. "What?"

248

"You heard me."

"You're lying."

"Am I now? Pity her *real* husband died. Not long after he heard news of your mother's death."

"Stop it. Stop lying to me!"

I didn't go out the back door. I walked out of the kitchen and into the living room and felt my mother's eyes on me, there in black in white, in her white nurse's cap, the photograph taken the day of her graduation from Toronto East General. She watched me move through the room. This man she'd married – Geordie – he couldn't be my father, my insides told me that, in knots and whirls and churning. Nana was lying. What Geordie did to her was there in my nightmare, the image of pus and scab and desperation, the corpse in the wedding dress reaching to grab me. The words from her morphined mouth when I sat by her deathbed: *Geordie, don't...stop it...* She needed help – that hand from my nightmare – she needed my help. What made me see this I couldn't say, but it was there, here, inside the silence as Mom's photograph watched me move through the room.

Caitlin, I'm always watching.

I drove down the street to be out of sight of the red brick house, and I parked the Malibu under a leafy maple tree. I stared at the *M* line on my shaking palm. *M* for *mother* and *M* for *Mary Ellen* but not for *marriage.*

Mom left him because he was abusive. She must've been pregnant with me. Was that it? She must've cheated on Geordie.

Nana had her money now – the money that helped finance her daughter's costly home care so she could stay at the quarry for as long as possible, the money I had to take out of my own inheritance to pay Nana back. She'd even charged me interest. And then I remembered the boxes in my trunk — the dolls and the Blue Willow dishes.

I knew little of Mom's childhood, snippets and fragments, but I knew Nana had used silence as a weapon. That day we drove home from the mall, so long ago, me and Mom and Eleanor, without the black bathing suit I wanted so badly, with the white nightgown instead — while I sulked in the back seat, Mom told Eleanor about that game she used to play with the neighbourhood children. "We'd pile rocks on the front lawn of the playmate we were mad at: limestone rocks, granite rocks, any rock would do. We'd pile them high to show our anger."

The Quarrel Game, Nana had called it.

Quarrel. Quarry.

I drove to Harrison Park, found as many as I could. I piled them in the back seat, the front seat, the trunk; they weighed the Malibu down, but when I put it into drive, it moved.

By the time I drove back to the red brick house, the dusk was turning day into darkness. Her curtains were drawn. I was safe.

It felt good being physical. Moving things from *A* to *B*. Shaping with my hands.

When I was done, I stood and wiped the dirt on my jeans, stepped back to see my efforts. There on the front lawn of the red brick house, beneath the shadow of the single pine tree, two boxes were stored safely inside my above-ground quarry. The family heirlooms Dad had wanted me to have so badly had turned toxic. The stones would speak more loudly than my shouts of anger.

The urge was there to smash the Blue Willow dishes one

by one, to pull apart the heads and limbs of the porcelain dolls — I'd almost done it — but when I saw the *m* line on my hand again, I saw the word *me*.

I recalled Mom's story of the Blue Willow. The Captain and Blue and the Handsome Man. This wasn't the original Chinese legend. She'd changed the original to connect the story to one she needed to tell.

"Doesn't the lie bother you?" Michael had said when I read him the story from the library book.

I'd thought hard about his question.

I could see her storytelling as a lie, a bend of the truth, or I could see it as a gift. Her mind had reformed the legend with pieces of her own life, the way myth blends real with imagined.

Both stories ended with birds, like the pair perched side by side on the telephone wire above my above-ground quarry — the outline at dusk of two mourning doves, feather tails shaped like matching arrows.

Water and Stone

WHEN I SAW THE QUARRY AGAIN, the bungalow was empty of life and the cedar walls were knotted with memories. I couldn't stay inside it any longer, so I went down to the dock and looked out at the water. The stillness doubled the enclosing landscape. When I looked down, I watched a water bug skate across the sun's red shimmer as if carrying its own reflection.

"I've let her down," Dad had said after she died. "This place was supposed to heal her."

The doctors had given Mom one more year after her "woman's operation." My parents hadn't planned on moving. Looking at houses for sale was a diversion, a kind of a lark. They liked living in Grimsby at the Upside-Down House. It suited them just fine. But then Dad saw Mom's face when she first saw the quarry, and he knew what he had to do – keep the light there.

She lived another year. And another. And another. She watched me grow from a pigtailed girl into a woman with breasts big enough to fill this white nightgown, the one I was wearing now, here on the dock. In that way, the quarry did heal her. For a time.

She turned to light when she died, as witnessed by my father. But she'd been turning to light even before she died – her thinning skin, luminous, like the light through a stained glass window, the light coming from inside her, a red core of fire through ice.

Michael remained my friend – what he'd been all along. My grieving body couldn't lie; it had always known the answer. He was sad at first. We both were. He'd always believed we could make things work, given time, our history, his role as protector. But once he admitted what my body had always known, his casual friendship with a male employee slowly turned to love. He'd denied his true nature. I'd been his excuse.

I wanted him to be happy. He deserved to be happy.

The top layer of the quarry water naturally turns for the dormant bottom. Things turn to be what they need to be.

I wanted to keep the professor in my life, but my pulling away had created a strange surge of energy in him. He'd call and hang up just to hear my voice. I knew it was him. One night, he left a message: *You need me, Caitlin. Can't you see that? Don't you know how I feel about you?*

I had always believed I needed a man – a father, a boy-friend, an older man – to show me who I was, who I was supposed to be. I thought back to Linda's words that day at the diner when she told me about her divorce: *It brought me back to myself. I didn't need a man.* She'd said it so freely, so confidently.

Did Linda ever regret meeting my father? To live in the cloak of an affair and the aftermath of the loss of a life partner couldn't have been easy for her. She was there for him – always there – I'd seen that. More than he was for her. Dad put me first after Mom's death. I became his new priority. Wrapped in his net, an invisible net, as invisible as the Grimsby hedge, as invisible as death.

Such thoughts weaving through me were the kind of insights I'd shared in a third-floor office under caring eyes, the place where I'd opened up to my deepest self. But our kiss had changed our transaction, our unspoken arrangement.

He wanted more.

I had thought *I* wanted more. The current that ran between us like a humming wire.

"We have something special," he'd said the last time I sat in his office. "You know that, don't you? Like your mother and father. They were meant to be together."

He rolled his chair forward and leaned in to kiss me. This time I turned away, as if my body controlled my mind.

He leaned back. His eyes on me, dark, disapproving. I couldn't take it. I got up from my chair, his chair, and grabbed hold of my knapsack. I was thankful for the heavy weight grounding me, another focus. I headed for the door.

"Wait," he said softly, in opposition to that dark look.

I turned. "I'm sorry," I said, and walked out.

The night of my last exam, my last night on Bond Street, he dropped by the basement apartment to hand me a draft of his soon-to-be published study. On the title page, my name below his. Our dynamic staring back at me from that paper. We stood in the dark by the streetlight at the end of the driveway, next to his car, beneath the big maple tree, amid the scent of damp earth.

Again, I read my name below his. *If I stay with you, it will always be like this.*

"What's wrong with you?" he said when he saw the look on my face. "Michael can't give you what you need, you know that. I can—"

"I can't. I—"

He grabbed back his paper. "You'll be alone then," he said.

"Then let me be alone."

I thought about this as I walked around the quarry, circling the lapping blue. I stepped off the limestone and into the goldenrod field. The grasses tickled my feet. Beads of red shone with the last rays of sunset. Wild strawberries. I plucked one and plopped it into my mouth.

Was the wedding mouse Mom's way of saying, *Honey, I'm here*? A sign she wanted me to marry, knowing the pain her marriage to Geordie had caused her? I knew what he did to her. My visit with Eleanor had confirmed my suspicions.

"Caitlin, all mothers have a past. Do you think she wanted to relive that pain by talking about it? She was in enough pain, and he was the cause of it. I truly believe that, though I never said that to your mother."

My stomach knotted. "How could she stay with someone who'd do that to her?"

"Hope. Her quiet hope kept her inside that marriage. *He'll change, he's better now.* And the pressure from Florence. Your father's love gave her the courage to get out."

I touched the cool cotton of my white nightgown, bruised

it red with berry juice. *Maharg.* It was fate. I thought of the mourning doves on the Blue Willow dishes, how the lovers had turned into birds. Yet, the mouse Mom had given me had no groom. She stood alone in her white-laced beauty.

Something shifted in the breeze. A hollow tube of transparent light, scaly to the touch but complete and intact. I imagined the moment the snake slipped out of the casing, the body's way of beginning.

Earlier that day, when I drove down Windmill Point Road, I had deliberately passed the shingle-roofed house where the drowned woman had lived. The curtains were drawn. The grass was uncut. Who lived there now? Anyone?

She'd tied a rope around her ankle, its end to a rock. I've been to the other side – there are no rocks. Only ledges like unplanned stairs on which to sit and watch the day lay her red blade. Did the woman haul the rock from our woods or from the back of her shingled house? And where did she learn to tie a rope around a rock? I don't think she wore a bathing suit. No. Heavy clothes, like the heavy water inside her, drowning the bones and the organs, making her think there was no way out but under.

Or maybe she wore a white nightgown.

I don't know who found her or how they could, given the stone's solid anchor, but water is home to the other gravity. Things rise. What's airborne falls. The surface is where everything meets.

The woman who drowned never got another chance. Her secrets went with her. And now the quarry cradles them.

The urge to disappear. Alcohol was the rope tied around Dad. The stone around his ankle, the overturning car. He wanted to die. *Desperate people do desperate things.*

I walked back toward the house and headed into the garage and took down the coil of rope on the top shelf. When I returned to the quarry's edge, I tossed it into the rowboat, pushed out from the limestone ledge and stepped in. The sun was gone now, and I could feel the dusk settling on my skin as I rowed toward the other side where water was deepest. The swallows I'd watched earlier had turned into bats, frantic flutters replacing graceful swoops. Flying creatures move in rhythm with the core of their being, the way they're meant to move.

I don't know how to move in this world anymore.

But here, in this rowboat, I knew. Stroke by stroke, I made my way across the quarry's skin. I entered its rhythm. And when I listened deeper, I heard the silence behind the rhythm.

It was Dr. Delio who'd told me how the decision becomes the release. The burden of life, lifted. He saw it on his father's face the morning he hung himself. *He never looked so happy. I try to focus on that. Instead of the guilt.*

That September afternoon, sitting with Dad on the dock, I'd witnessed freedom on his face. Why else would he have mentioned a will? And yet, there was no will...

The bungalow was far away now. With no lights on, it merged with the darkness. I rowed on. I was almost there. I knew which rock I would use. It would be heavy enough.

I remembered how I used to swim across the quarry. I wasn't a fast swimmer. I would never win a race, but I had stamina.

Something startled me. A form in the overgrowth of bush. It was a great blue heron wading at the water's edge. Its long, elegant neck arched like a hill, its beak pointed downward.

All of life is a bend of the truth, the curve in the question mark.
I let go of the oars and let the boat slow.

The last heron I'd encountered was the dead one I'd found after Cindy had left the quarry. How long ago was that? Too long. I recalled how sad I was that day. The thought of it angered me. I had both parents then. Mom was sick, yes, but she was alive. Dad, too. And then I felt them both here, in the space between where I sat and the heron stood. Like a line of rope. I could feel the tug. And then a cutting feeling came with words, *leave it alone, row home.*

I dunked in the oars, turned around, and through the quiet, I rowed home.

THE HOUSE WAS EMPTY NOW. Ready and clean for the new owners. I stood in the kitchen looking out at the light-studded water, past the dock where my aunt sat waiting for me. The letter we'd read earlier was still in my hand. I hadn't expected this. I had been ready to exhume my mother's body, cremate them both, Rusty and Don, and scatter their ashes over the quarry. But given this letter from Nana, they'd have their last wish. All we needed now was the footmarker's inscription:

Donald Richard Maharg
beloved of
Mary Ellen Maharg

I joined my aunt on the dock bench.

"You've worked so hard, Caitlin. Summa cum laude. Such an accomplishment." She squeezed my knee like Dad used to do. "They'd be so proud." Her brown eyes watered.

She'd driven down the busy highway, the speedy truck-packed QEW, so it was more than the forecast of heavy snow that had stopped her from coming to our house that Christmas Day, so long ago, my uncle unable to drive because of his squash accident, his one arm in a sling. With no other way for the family to get to the quarry, the forecast of a winter storm had served its purpose, had given an excuse.

Or so I thought.

He'd been drinking when he dropped by their house in Burlington, mid-December, on his way home from the Toronto office of Dominion Envelope. More animated than usual. More lively. She could smell it on his breath. She could see it in his eyes.

After he finished the instant coffee she made for him, he got up from the kitchen chair to leave. Cindy, now home from school, needed a drive to her flute lesson. It was snowing and blowing outside, and the building was on his way, and he was leaving now anyway.

"I'll take her. Come on," he'd said, taking hold of Cindy's hand.

"No." Aunt Doris grabbed her daughter's other hand.

It got ugly then. That's what she said, and she wouldn't tell me more, only that he got in his car, the Seville, and drove away.

There were other stories, but I'd heard enough. I'd had enough.

"She kept him in line, your mother. The only one he'd listen to." She shook her head. "But she couldn't always be there."

I thought about the accident on Stonemill Road. There was a deer. There wasn't a deer.

Not knowing was the ultimate answer. To live in the mystery of water and stone.

"You only graduate once," she said. "And you're the first in our family."

A soft wind made the water flutter.

"They won't be there." The waves subsided. "Why bother?"

"Honey, not physically. Look, I'm not a churchgoer. I'm not a religious person, but I do feel there's more to us than meets the eye. You *are* your parents. You're the physical embodiment of Don and Rusty." She smiled. "Besides, your uncle and I will be there. Cindy and the boys. It's up to you."

She stood up from the dock bench. I saw my father. The tilt of his body.

"Linda, too?"

"Of course, dear. All who love you."

I warmed to the word: *love.*

Aunt Doris shook her head. "It wasn't easy for your parents. Divorce wasn't easy back then. Spouses had to publicize their intent in newspapers, including details—can you imagine?—then petition the government to let them go their separate ways. Grounds of cruelty came in only after you were born." She paused. "They should've told you they weren't legally married. Not Florence. I'm sorry you had to go through that." She turned to look at me. "But your father was your father. *Is* your father."

"I know. I've always known that. Her lie couldn't shake me."

When the clouds shifted, the quarry glowed blue again. It would always change and return to change.

"I'll go," I said. Then I got down on my stomach and leaned over the edge of the dock. I poked my reflection with my ring finger and watched the ripples ring out.

Acknowledgements

Quarry came into being over a period of many years. Key in helping shape early versions of the manuscript were Marilyn Bowering, Alistair MacLeod, Barbara Berson and Allyson Latta. Invaluable feedback came from Kelli Deeth, Ibi Kaslik and Ken Murray. I couldn't possibly list individually all the other people who have contributed in various ways, but you know who you are, and I thank you.

Gratitude to Stacey May Fowles and Megan Griffith-Greene for publishing "Red Bars" in *She's Shameless*, Emily Schultz for publishing "Three in a Room" in *Joyland Magazine* and Kathryn Mockler for publishing "Special" in *Joyland Magazine*.

Thanks to Kate Domina for her haunting painting "Lone Doe" and to Natalie Olsen of Kisscut Design for the stunning cover.

Lastly, I would like to extend deepest thanks to my multi-talented editor and publisher, Alexandra Leggat, for her vision and commitment to bringing *Quarry* to life. She (and her two wolves!) made the dream happen.

"Dive in. Turn to water before it freezes." is from my poem "Back to the Quarry" in *Pupa* (Insomniac Press).

"I know, I know. How long have I known? Or have I always known, in some far crevice of my heart, some cave too deeply buried, too concealed?" is from *The Stone Angel* by Margaret Laurence (McClelland & Stewart).

The definition of *orgasm* is from *Webster's New World Dictionary, Second College Edition*, s.v. "orgasm."

CATHERINE GRAHAM is the author of six acclaimed poetry collections, including *Her Red Hair Rises with the Wings of Insects*, a finalist for the Raymond Souster Award and the CAA Poetry Award. She received an Excellence in Teaching Award at the University of Toronto School of Continuing Studies, where she teaches creative writing. She was also the winner of the International Festival of Authors' Poetry NOW. While living in Northern Ireland, Graham completed an M.A. in Creative Writing from Lancaster University. Her work has appeared in journals and anthologies around the world. *Quarry* is her first novel. Visit her at **www.catherinegraham.com**.

Author Photo Credit: Portrait Boutique